Bastion

- A novel by Rambaro Pellegrino -

The weak are dominated by the strong. The strong are being ruled by the intellectual ones. The cunning reign over all. And the wise? The wise observe with coot how everything crumbles down again…

The grandmaster of Meriva

Contents

A New Cycle

'Star... Do you want to come down? Please, come down if you want...'

'Yes! Wait up!'

Star hurriedly packs her leather pouch. She gathers the new writing tubes and charcoal fillings she had acquired, and before she forgets, she also takes the fresh parchment scroll she recently received from her grandfather.

She slowly runs her fingers over the leather surface of the bag, 'Thank you dear cow,' is what she says. Star then quickly looks through the wooden interior to see if she hasn't forgotten something.

I'll try to be a little nicer to grandpa, the coming period, is what she thinks to herself as she walks through the wooden room. He always does his best for me, so... Now again, with giving me these things. I'll also try to whine a little less when I have to do some odd job again.

Star gazes at her reflection in a flat ceramic plate with a layer of water on it. *I'm going for it this cycle!* is what she enthusiastically thinks as she splashes some water out of the plate with her hand.

But even though there is the will to do things very differently this cycle, her true interest really lies elsewhere. And Star stands still for a moment in front of the small window opening of her bedroom. Because if it were up to her, she wouldn't go to the learning bench at all. No, instead she would immerse herself completely in that great wide wilderness out there. That wide green expanse that lay in front of her from behind this window opening; a forest that reaches as far as the eye can see. Because, what could actually be out there? And, what mysteries are waiting for her there? Just thinking about it makes her restless.

Someday, she may unravel the secrets of that forest landscape out there, but until then, she will have to behave as neatly as possible, be the best possible woman-human there is, and try to adhere to the rules of her community as best as she can. *I know I have it in me!* Star jumps up with a cat leap, in which the tubes in her pouch rattling happily—sounds that remind her of the valuables she carries with her...

With wild dance moves, and as effectively as she can, she tries to get rid of the buildup tension within her body. There is no one watching anyway...

She looks at the plate with water once more, and then speaks some encouraging words to herself: 'You can do this Star! Try to keep the appeal of the forest and the discipline of the community as separate as possible. That little piece of forest is yours, and yours only. No one needs to know of it. Not even grandpa!' And Star winks at her own reflection. 'Every creature has the right to push its limits, to explore its boundaries, no matter what they say...'

A vibrant feeling rushes through her for a moment, but at the same time also a different kind of realization, and she sighs deeply. *I have to restrain myself...*

The pouch dangles happily at her side as Star walks

with fast paces toward the community center. It's already busy in the large courtyard, and a big group of knowledge-takers is present. One of the elders stands on a high platform while he tries to calm down the noisy crowd.

Oops! is what Star has to think. *It looks like I'm a little too late for the recitation of the precepts this cycle*, and she joins the group as inconspicuously as possible. And even though it seems that her lateness hasn't been noticed by one of the elders, that remains to be seen...

Star listens with pricked-up ears to the rules of community conduct that one of the elders now begins to recite:

'Silence! Underlings! I demand complete silence from you! From all of you! We, as elders, understand the excitement that this special news brings. And it is, together with the arrival of a new cycle, indeed highly exceptional...

But! That doesn't give you any right to forget about the precepts of the previous cycle! Let alone those of the ever-valid senate!'

It suddenly becomes very quiet on the square, and a few people seem to get a slight blush on their faces by hearing these words.

Star, and many with her, then listen with a serious expression to what their community leader has to say to them:

'Well, where was I...? As I tried to indicate earlier, we now have a newcomer in our midst: just step forward Thomias...'

Star looks excitedly at her fellow spectators for a

moment, while she finds it difficult to keep her composure and not to immediately ask about the who, the what, or the why.

She already stands on all her toes when the front group shifts back and forth, and a man-boy steps forward to stand next to the elder on the platform...

'Dear novices, knowledge-takers, and also residents of our magnificent community!

May I introduce you to this permanent resident within Alfalfa?! This is Thomias, a man-boy from the Betanex community. Because of an expansion within the various communities, it is necessary that we accommodate both him and his family in our community section. So give this man-boy a chance to get used to our infrastructure. As you have learned during the previous cycle, it is only possible to travel between these communities by means of a certificate of approval, or by means of a certificate of exception, and so via permission to travel.

And that's why... and we think you will understand that... he and his family are automatically familiar with the codes of behavior and conduct that apply within our community...'

A fellow novice, standing next to Star, puts up a questioning face for a moment, and Star also seems to have forgotten much of what they had learned in the previous cycle. *Because, how did one obtain a certificate of approval again?* She'll really have to pay more attention if she wants to be a good novice and therefore also a full-fledged underling.

'We wish both you and your family a peaceful and

pleasant stay within our splendid community. We hope that you'll find your place as quietly and as peacefully as possible, although we as elders have full confidence in that.

Something that seems to be true for most of us, however, and unfortunately, not applicable to all...' And the elder let his gaze glide over the crowd for a moment, and even seemed to stop at Star's face.

'Okay, that was that,' was what he finally said. 'For the rest, you are in luck, that the regulations have remained largely the same this cycle. However, don't let this be a reason for renunciation! Our system is completely based on cooperation. There rests a great responsibility on you as residents, and therefore, at the same time, a responsibility on the community as a whole.

May we be spared problems as much as possible this cycle, and let our quality of life and our workings be as fruitful as always. With this, we are wishing you a prosperous cycle. You may go now...

Or... No! Wait! Before we forget, and perhaps most important of all...

Since an age, changes have been made within the codes of the senate; this in view of a sudden expansion of our habitat and a number of other things.

This will mean, in layman's talk, that certain laws will fall away and others will take their place. However, we will pay further attention to this during the novice's system. So those who, for example, have already forgotten about the guidelines for obtaining proof of approval are in luck. Although, I don't know if you can count yourself lucky if you are afflicted with a lazy character or forgetful traits...'

Star wipes away some rising sweat from her forehead. How astute those elders always are... It's quite coincidental that he exactly mentioned that guideline that I was just thinking about.

Star had heard people occasionally suggest that the elders possess certain special gifts. And some souls even dare to claim that they can see into the future or read the minds of others...

Could the man have done that to her a moment ago? Had the elder just read her own thoughts? Or was this simply due to coincidence?

Those elders remain a mystery to me... is what Star thinks when she almost doesn't dare to look the man in the face anymore.

They are always so ad rem, so pertinent. I always get a bad taste in my mouth from their speeches. They are always so... so compelling...!

But fortunately, Star didn't come into contact with them too often...

'Grandpa! You know you can use your rest, don't you?! You are already doing enough around here, aren't you?!'

Grandpa Maxwell had just walked into their wooden shelter, slouching and mumbling...

The spiral treehouse that Star and Grandpa Maxwell live in is one of the largest within Alfalfa, and Star doesn't know why that is exactly, although it's probably due to Grandpa's industry through the many cycles. The man is always busy with something, for as long as Star can remember, and she looks at him as he stands there so helplessly at a distance.

The man already enters his eighth era... Which means that he has completed at least seventy cycles already. *Gosh...* is what Star has to think. That alone is an achievement in itself...

'Can you please help me, Star? If you want to, that is...'

'Yes! Wait a minute! I'm on my way!' is what she shouts back for the umpteenth time. Star relaxedly grabs some bottled juice from the cool water-filled tub, and then walks to the back of their round treehouse while she takes the interior within her gaze.

He even made this spiral house; a completely carved-out tree with a ground floor and two floors above. Along the inside of the tree, a wooden staircase spirals up, and thus passes through both floors during its climb. Star's private room is located on the second floor... *Real female-humans live on top!* is what she has to think to herself with a laugh, even though it doesn't really make sense. Her head starts to feel dizzy when she has to think of all the work that had to be done in carving out this house. Because its creation alone lasted many cycles, if she is to believe her grandfather.

Although, the man must have had help from others, it can hardly be otherwise...

When Star walks outside, she sees how Grandpa is once again busy in the vegetable garden adjacent to their treehouse. The man looks up for a moment when he sees Star approaching.

'How did it go today? Are you back already? Or has time gone so fast this revolution?!' Her grandfather looks around confused and seems to be looking for his time-indicator. And while the man continues to search further, Star answers his questions with patience:

'Yes, it went quite well, actually. Only a few new rules of conduct have been implemented this cycle. And that's why I'm home a bit earlier. And...

Oh, yes! A new man-boy from Betanex has arrived. Very exciting! Have you heard about that?'

'From Betanex, you say?' The man looks at the time-indicator in his old wrinkled hand while this question leaves his mouth in a mumbling way. And Star decides to take a good look at the man again, as he sits there bent over in their vegetable garden, although it is not without concern. Her grandfather is getting really old now. And even though the man tries to appear strong, he seems to be needing her care now more than ever...

'Can you perhaps see what is written on here?' And with squinted eyes, he hands Star the small time-indicator. However, Star had to laugh a little inside. The thing isn't even adjusted for today, and it's even set on two revolutions ago...

'Well! Isn't that nice!' is what her grandpa suddenly shouts. 'Now I also need some looking glasses...!'

The man gets up frustrated, after which he slowly picks up the gardening tools. *But grandpa! I can do such things! Now can't I?!* Star snatches the tools ferociously from his old hands, although at the same time, a kind of guilt creeps up on her as soon as she has a hold of the objects. And even though she means it all well, she could also bring it with some more tact… She turns to him with a smile: 'Grandpa, you know you can use your rest, don't you? Surely you are already doing enough around here, aren't you?'

And she decides to repeat the question as grandpa's hearing continues to deteriorate, while he, on top of that, is also starting to become forgetful.

The man then shuffles around their accommodation, mumbling.

It's probably getting harder for him by the day… is what Star has to think for a moment. It's probably becoming increasingly difficult for him not to play a key role in this whole community life anymore…

But when his mood has improved a bit, Star will once again call on his knowledge; something that always does him visibly good, and so does it Star. Because, and as always, this female human, this underling, and also this freshly new novice, has a lot to ask him…

It's already a bit later when Grandpa Maxwell and Star are sitting calmly around a crackling fire. The wood sparks fly in various directions, and Star knows how to follow them with her gaze; along the spiral staircase and towards the open roof vault. Some of these light sparks even manage to escape through the hole before disappearing from view again. *Actually… lives are just like that…* is what Star suddenly has to think. *One being seems to propel unhindered, up and beyond their chosen and taken path, with an inexhaustible life force and chased by that which must be Lady Luck. While other beings may be fortunate if they even become a spark at all, and even then they don't have to leave the hearth of origin…*

They may fly in a certain direction, but before they realize it they'll fade out; completely at the mercy of circumstances that hinder their free flight...

Star goes back in her mind and to her parents, whom she had never known, or at least, whom she cannot remember. Short-term sparks were whatever they were. *But why? And why both?* Tears well up in her eyes, although she quickly wipes them away before grandpa can see them.

'Grandpa?'

'Yes, sweetheart?'

'Why are the village elders so strict? I mean... I love community life, and I understand very well that our rules have to be enforced, but why does it have to be done with such a stern hand? Because, whenever I come back from the f... Ehm, from the beautiful nature that is so present in our community, I notice a certain feeling of happiness. But as soon as the wise elders come up with their strict rules, they immediately seem to nullify that experience.

They propagate the natural beauty, and also the serenity within the community, but at the same time it seems as if enjoying it to the fullest is forbidden. At least, that's the impression I get from them. Why can't all be a bit looser?'

The old man shifts in his bamboo seat, while at the same time clearing his throat; a second sign that a serious message is coming Star's way:

'Are you at it again, Star? We've already talked about this subject, haven't we?'

But Star feels a frustration rising for a moment.

'What do you mean?!' is what she asks.

'About the fact that the elders are so shady?! Or that I should never talk about anything that concerns me at all?!'

But now it's her grandpa who seems to be getting angry.

'Not so rude, Star! Because you know damn well what I'm referring to!'

And yes, indeed, you shouldn't immerse yourself so much as far as the elders are concerned. They know very well what they are doing. They are sensible people. And you could learn a lot from their wisdom. You'd better focus on this cycle, because the previous one didn't go so well either. You've barely made it to the novice level. And given the cycles you already have behind you, that's the least to be expected from you...' However, Star decided not to wait for the words that were always served as so-called sweet delicacies to her in this home. No, instead, she flees the spiral treehouse and decides to walk around the community grounds. But while she stares at the ground somewhat, or sometimes looks at some other shelters, she notices that grandpa's words have had a certain hold on her; at least, more than expected. Yet, she just can't understand why he always has to behave like this; sometimes so sweet and then again so curt when it comes to the community rules, to the codes of the senate, or both.

If he only knows what really drives her, although she would probably never be able to talk to him about it. While at the same time always expecting her to take care of him. Because, even though Star always keeps a nice face, she actually hates that task. Actually, Star only wants one thing out of life: Star really and only just wants to be free... Another tear wells up, and all her grievances seem to resurface again: Missing her parents, whom she had never known. Taking care of the old man who happens to be her grandfather, but with whom she seems to share a love-hate relationship. Of course, Alfalfa's strict hassle; a community of which she is also a part. But above all, her own character; a character that always seems to get in her way. Why isn't she as stable as everyone else? She goes crazy over her fickle behavior. For now, try to focus on this cycle, Star! It's just the way it is! Yes... indeed... it's just the way it is...

When Star returns to her shelter, Grandpa Maxwell has already gone to his nest. Now, it will not be long before the lights go out again, and then this revolution will also be over. But just before Star goes to her own nest, she decides to go through the knowledge that has been taught to them in the previous cycle. She looks at the notes that describe her chosen industry, and she also writes down a number of standard things that she could discuss with the newcomer, with the new male-boy, if she dares to confront him at least...

Okay, what was it again? Oh yes, one cycle is three hundred revolutions, and one revolution is once light and once darkness. Multiple cycles are called eras of course, and what else is there? Gosh, I've really forgotten a lot... Perhaps it's better to concentrate on my chosen industry for now... Perhaps it's better to leave things as they are for a while...

The Community Temple

The first ten revolutions are progressing steadily. Star sits quietly in the learning-bench and tries to immerse herself as much as possible in the knowledge that comes her way, and in her chosen industry, an industry that fortunately lies close to her heart. The male-boy from Betanex, who is called Thomias by everyone, sits only a seat away. And even though Star regularly has the feeling that he is staring at her, or that he even seems to be looking for a certain approach, she manages to fend off this inclination for the time being... She doesn't really understand why she's the target of his interest. And even though she doesn't find it annoying, and it even strokes her ego somewhat, she simply doesn't know if it's wise to hook up with this male-boy from Betanex.

Because, even though the new cycle has only just started, she already seems to be drowning in all the learning-bench work. And her real aim for now is to really seize her industry during this cycle, during these three hundred revolutions.

She will have to continue to do her best, for both herself and grandpa, both in the learning bench as well as on the home front. Moreover, she also has her hobby that she wants to pay attention to, so once in a while, even if it isn't, if she is to believe the community rules, entirely allowed.

And then, of course, there is also what no one knows

about her, and what Star prefers not to talk about, because this could put both her and grandpa in a bad spotlight. It is something which makes Star very nervous, but which, at the same time, makes her heart beat faster… And if Star wants to keep up with this busy schedule, it will be very difficult to make time for a new friend. Who knows, perhaps later, maybe later, but for now, probably better not…

When the apprenticeship is finished during that revolution, Star decides to walk through the community on her own, something she does almost every revolution. She sees how many an underling is busy with his or her personally chosen industry. Some people, especially the female-humans, know how to weave together the most beautiful and most user-friendly objects; an industry that Star would also love to practice. What many female-people have also chosen in their novice time is the processing of animal skins; skins that they know how to cut into pieces and that they use to make clothing, for large tarpaulins that possibly can be used as a tent, but also for handy small bags in which herbs can be stored, for example.

And of course they also make the—so characteristic for Alfalfa—bigger pouch-bags, one as Star also carries over her shoulder. Star has therefore been hesitating for a long time between these two industries. But when her love for her 'forbidden hobby' began to grow, the conviction for her choice also became stronger. Star had already made her choice, had made up her mind about it, and felt a certain peace for it…

Star walks a bit further while she sees what the man-people are doing.

They are industries that she has seen practiced at least hundreds of times, if not more, and for which she has developed a great respect because these industries also know how to keep their community running. She sees for the umpteenth time how these man-people are furiously busy with pieces of flint, while manufacturing them with precision into handy tools. Some of them build temporary—or permanent—huts from the materials available in and around Alfalfa. And of course, there are the man-people who spend their time toiling on the land and who are therefore engaged in growing crops.

Even with Star's grandfather, Grandfather Maxwell, it seems that he has never been able to completely let go of this industry. Because, even though the man is entering his eighth era, there doesn't seem to be a revolution going by without him being found in their communal vegetable garden.

Star pleasantly walks past the man and woman-people, and greets them in a friendly way, or waves back, when someone looks up from his or her work.

But Star isn't just strolling meaningless during this revolution. Her steps are also taking her to a building that she hasn't paid a visit to for a very long time.

She stands in front of the pearly white building for a moment and then limps a bit nervously on both legs. The building with its beautifully carved out pillars of natural stone and with the round dome at the top of it, which many underlings look at in awe because they still don't exactly know how it was made, or who actually had the skill to build it... And Star also stares at this imposing structure for a short time in that way.

Because, what would it be like to live in such a building? And, how stately would one feel about that? The building that Star is admiring is known to the residents of Alfalfa as the community temple, a structure open to and intended for everyone, and in which one can move freely. It is the backbone of the community; a free zone where, for example, detailed information can be found about the industries that one would like to master. It houses a doctor where one can go for pains or worse injuries, and it is also the place where the elders themselves reside. Where one can find the codes of conduct of the ever-valid senate, and one can also go for a proof of approval, a certificate that an underling needs to have to be able to travel between the different communities...

But even though Star used to come here almost every revolution, that seems to have become less and less since the last cycle. The temple has become a building that she feels less and less comfortable in. As if she's being observed by several eyes. As if she's constantly being watched by something or someone. And this seems to make her feel more and more nervous and anxious...

Nevertheless, Star has always been eager to learn; curious about the new implemented codes of the senate, and also curious about the knowledge that an obedient underling must know of within this community, within this society, if one wants to be able to fully belong. But, she is of course also curious about the rooms where the elders reside… Yet, it seems that her eagerness to learn about these community rules has shifted to the exercise of her forbidden passion. It's almost as if the elders have been purposely making it difficult for her lately. She feels that consciously, somehow, and it starts to crawl under her skin.

It makes Star more and more tense nowadays, while feeling less and less at home. She feels less and less like a full-fledged underling, and this seems to make her lonelier and sadder...

Star walks tensely into the community temple, hoping that she won't bump into any elders, and hoping that she can do her own thing with ease, and that no annoying questions will follow. She pauses for a moment at a mural; a fresco that had always fascinated her and continues to do so now.

It is a story that everyone in Alfalfa knows about and probably many in other communities as well. The mural tells the tragic tale of the Great War; an event that, according to the elders, took place more than ten eras ago.

The two largest communities: Deltarion and Epsilonia, had been fighting for absolute power at that time. Two families that apparently stood directly opposite to each other, and who didn't want to budge or give away ground.

But the other three communities: Betanex, Gammanon, and Alfalfa itself, also started to get involved in this dispute. Chaos was, of course, what followed; many people had died among the violence, and eventually the communities had to be completely rebuilt from the ground up. That was the point, the crucial moment, that the elders came forward to apply their structure and their rules of conduct. Because, even though the elders may have been strict and adamant, such a thing should of course never ever happen again.

According to Grandpa Maxwell, their strictness served to protect the communities, and thus of course also their inhabitants, their underlings.

Many stories circulate about that time, and many myths and sagas have arisen about it, but no one knows exactly how it all happened or the exact time when it occurred. What everyone does agree on is the following:

The Great War either arose because people couldn't deal with a certain form of power, or it arose from a form of discontent, but probably from a combination of both...

Star still stares mesmerized at the fresco when she's startled by a figure that suddenly stands behind her. When she turns around, she is shocked blankly. It is one of the elders! However, the man decides to say nothing while staring at the plaque on the wall underneath the fresco with a big grin. Should Star say anything to him? Should she do nothing at all? Or should she just walk away quietly? Quickly back to grandpa and to their spiral tree home again? One of the few places where she can still relax a bit?

She observes the man as he stands there so quietly, while at the same time admiring the clothes that characterize him so much.

The man wears a long robe, has leather sandals on his feet that no one else is allowed to wear, and he is decked out with decorations and ornaments that an average person could never ever come into contact with. She looks the man in the face for a moment, although he continues to stare at the plaque beneath the mural in silence. When Star tries to walk away silently, and when she's almost at the entrance and wants to descend the grand staircase, she is, to her horror, called back by the elder...

'Dear Star! I would like you to come back and stand next to me for a while...'

Star does what she's told and walks back in silence. The man still keeps his eyes on the engraved text when he speaks to the young Star: 'Star... Were you once again looking at this fresco? Do you really find it that interesting? Come, young novice, tell me what your opinion is on this piece of history...' But Star suddenly feels a nervousness looming, although she also knows that she can't show it too openly, as it's considered a form of weakness, according to the elders. And on top of that, it may also imply that she has something to hide. And even though that's of course the case, the elders are absolutely not allowed to know about it. She tells him her vision of the Great War as concentrated as possible; just as any other underling would do in her position.

The only unorthodox thing she does say is that she seems to feel a certain fascination for it, and that she would like to know what caused that pandemonium exactly. At the same time, she also tries to come up with an excuse for her actual visit to this temple; that she came to get a new piece of fool's gold, simply because theirs is used up...

The man looks at her attentively for a moment, but decides not to go into depth about it, at least not for now... 'You have a curious disposition, Star,' is what the man suddenly says, while he keeps his gaze fixed on the fresco.

'Many may dare to claim that the Great War was caused by a certain craving for power, or something that arose from a certain form of discontent, but we as elders share our own opinion of that. In our opinion, it is therefore, and for now it may be a bit simplified, 'originated out of a certain form of curiosity...'

The dissatisfaction may have been present at the time, but we as elders think it was the urge to want to know more, to want to know about everything, that initially fueled this disaffection. One must be satisfied with one another, whatever community they live in, or do you perhaps disagree with that sometimes, Star?' The man still doesn't look at her directly but puts his big hand on her shoulder, sometimes even touching her neck for a moment.

Star cringes a bit because of this, even if it's not because of this fleeting male contact. It's because of what she wears around her neck and what the elder is absolutely not allowed to find out. Why, for crying out loud, did she have to wear the thing around her neck today? Dumb, very dumb, even extremely thoughtless... Star says affably that she appreciates being able to live in a community like this one, and says somewhat veiled that she very well understands what the elder is referring to...

The elder takes his hand off her shoulder and looks at her directly this time, although it's Star now who keeps her eyes on the drawing on the wall.

The man seems to be worried about something, although Star doesn't really understand about what. When the man walks away, he asks her another question in his steps: 'Haven't you forgotten something,

Star?' But Star had no idea what he could be referring to. 'You came here for a chunk of fool's gold, didn't you? Which was gone, lost, oh no, was used up, wasn't it?'

Star feels a blush appearing on her cheeks while looking at the ground, somewhat embarrassed. 'That's... that's right, sir,' is what she stammers.

The elder walks with a controlled manner into his room, comes back almost instantly, and then puts the piece of pyrite in her hand. He then looks at her intently.

'You do understand, Star, that fool's gold can't just perish, don't you? That it can't just dissolve into nothingness...? That it can't just be used up...?'

The man walks back into his room, and Star manages to shout something after him before he closes the door: 'I'm sorry! We've lost it! I... I didn't know how else to bring it...' But the door was already closed... Nevertheless, a voice sounded from behind the door; a muffled voice that spoke directly to Star and made her neck hairs stand up immediately: 'Star... Sweet little Star... Please don't try to become a forest wanderer...'

Star sits all alone in her room towards the middle of that revolution. And she even feels more alone now, even more alone than ever before. Why did the elder say that to her? And why that particular sentence? Star touches her chest and feels the pendant resting under her vest. She pulls up the string around her neck and looks at the symbol as she has done so many times before, so many times before, all alone in her bedroom; there deep and high atop in the ridge of their wooden spiral treehouse... *Would the elder perhaps know about it? Had he perhaps felt the string around her neck? That thin piece of rope, when he had put his hand on her shoulder at the community temple?* It has been a long time since she received this pendant from her grandpa. A gift that surprised her because no one in Alfalfa, or in any other community for that matter, was allowed to distinguish oneself through such decorations on the body. That was simply stated in the rules of conduct, and even in the codes of the senate:

One shouldn't distinguish him or herself from any other underlying by physical finery...

She knew this sentence all too well... But once grandpa had told her the real story behind this pendant, she had no other choice but to carry it with her all the time, well hidden under her clothes. It was simply the only thing she still owned of her mother; a woman she had never really known, but who was always somewhat close by in this way... Star wistfully puts her face in her hands. She feels tears coming up again, but doesn't know whether to control them or to let them run free. *Is it really that bad what I'm doing?* Is what she asks herself. *Am I really that rebellious at heart? Am I just like all those other discontented people? All those other curious ones? Who caused the Great War due to their inconsiderate dispositions and their insubordination?*

She kisses the wooden pendant, tucks it tightly under her vest, and then tries to fall asleep while the light from outside immediately goes dark...

The Mysterious Object

There is no learning-bench, the next revolution, and Star decides to occupy herself with her forbidden hobby that day. Actually, she doesn't care much what the other underlings think of it, and what the elders might think of it, would they ever found out. She's actually not doing anything wrong at all. And if the elders do decide to talk to her about it, then she at least will have her word ready. It will be for the benefit of the community as a whole, everyone could benefit from it, and not a word would be lied about.

Star walks around the spiral treehouse, looks around to make sure no one sees her, and then disappears through the bushes. She knows the checkpoints, because she always keeps a close eye on them. And she also roughly knows where the first checkpoint is located and where the guards are probably walking around... Star walks through the green surroundings for a while, while she slowly starts to come back to herself. She walks along the many colored flowers, along the bushes with those delicious yellow curved fruits hanging from them, along the thin crooked trees from which she will get her braiding material in the future, and of course, along the shrub that she likes best, and that grows in and around Alfalfa in many numbers. She therefore runs her hand over the leaf that is known to the locals as the divergent feathered leaf bush. Star feels connected to this piece of greenery in some way. The shrub can be found in large numbers, but on the other hand stands solitary on the ground, just like Star herself actually does. Moreover, the shrub is always beautifully green-colored and seems to enjoy the many other plant species that surround it, just like Star experiences the lush green surroundings around her. The large leaves look a bit like the feathers of a bird, hence the name. Star is now completely in her element, and the many crawling, flying, and climbing animals and insects around her seem to contribute to this. Star just can't understand that there can be someone who can't appreciate these natural apparitions. Star walks a bit further while the geckos, the tarantulas, the green tree snakes, and the hummingbirds climb, crawl, and fly around her hastily. Walking around in this lush area has done her good, and so she walks back into Alfalfa whistling in satisfaction again. She feels like doing something this particular revolution, even feels an urge for 'green fingers', and before she knows it, she sits with both knees in the vegetable garden that she shares with her grandfather.

Star was reminded of something for a moment, somewhere in the middle of the previous revolution, when she lay alone on her nest and looked at the pendant she had once received from her grandfather; a gesture he didn't have to make, because it could've earned them many crooked looks from the other residents within their community. Nevertheless, he had decided to give her the hanger anyway, simply because he knew how important it would be to her. And whenever Star thought about that for a moment—the risk that the man had taken by doing so—she felt the urge to do something for him in return. And very often that resulted in making a good meal for him; just to get through the following revolution safe and sound… Star, therefore, looks at the crops that had supplemented their diet so often. She sees the yellow curved fruit, which tastes so nice and sweet, and that she, just a moment ago, and not too far outside of Alfalfa, saw growing in all its splendor. She sees the small, green, and slightly curved fruit, which is super healthy, but makes their meal always a pot of slime. She looks at the fluffy plant that she occasionally brings to the neighbor because that woman-human is very capable of turning it into yarn. And then, of course, at the variety of tubers and small groundnuts that gave both her and grandpa such a satiated stomach. Star puts a finger to her lips and then thinks for a moment. *What will I surprise grandpa with this time? In any case, the plant that bears the sweet tubers already looks fine around this time of the cycle… Shall I take the chance? Shall I surprise grandpa with a sweet tuber jar? Sprinkled with some pink pepper? And perhaps even with a piece of goat meat on the side? Then again, the piece of meat probably has to wait for now,* is what she thinks, while she looks at the tuber plant mesmerized. According to Grandpa Maxwell, this was all men's work. And by that, he mainly meant the work of planting these tubers into the deep, dark soil. According to him, nothing else gave underlings blacker fingernails. No, this definitely wasn't a job for a novice, let alone for an ordinary female-girl! But Star wasn't just a novice, and certainly not just any female-girl. Throughout the cycles, Star had become familiar with the plants, with the shrubs, and, of course, with the trees that grew in the wider area. Moreover, she was very good at judging whether something was edible or not, even if some parts were poisonous. She seemed to have a keen eye for that. And if a woman-human could weave a beautiful basket; made of sturdy, hardened branches that they had to take out of the trees themselves sometimes, they surely could plant a sweet tuber?!

Star sniffed her nose. *It must be a view of the old days...* And she started digging ferociously. But as enthusiastically as she'd started the job, how more and more difficult it seemed to become. This indeed required a lot of muscle power, and the tubers lay much deeper in the ground than initially expected.

She also understood that the many worms and other teeming creatures that came crawling out of the ground could scare off a light-hearted woman-human. But Star had become familiar with these little creatures and even though she preferred not to say it aloud, perhaps because she was a bit ashamed of this silly fact, she considered these small insects also a bit as her friends...

Star decides to concentrate on the digging, just to get an indication of how far these 'vegetable arms' actually extended. She dug and dug, and kept on digging, although the constant falling back of the soil into the hole in the ground didn't really contribute to all the work. She quickly wiped some sweat from her forehead; an action that caused black streaks across her face. She almost wanted to give up, almost... But, because she found this all quite interesting, and she— and one of the elders had already mentioned this—had a curious disposition smoldering deep within her, she quickly looked around to see if she perhaps could find a tool for the digging. She walked into the treehouse, came back with an ivory soup spoon, and then continued with the digging part.

Star was now close to a tuber, she could barely feel it, but it had to be close. She followed the sturdy root deeper and deeper, she dug harder and harder, and then... And then a scraping sound followed... As if this tool of bone had stumbled upon something hard and massive. *Could it be a stone perhaps? It could hardly be otherwise... But a stone so deep in the ground? Could it perhaps be a very special stone? Or maybe even a piece of fool's gold? Or perhaps even a chunk of real gold?!*

Star's heart began to beat faster because of these thoughts, and she hoped and preferred for a piece of fool's gold; just so she didn't have to knock on the door of those sour elders anymore for the next few cycles... But when Star had managed to uncover a piece of the object, it didn't turn out to be a stone at all, or gold, or pyrite, or anything that looked like those things, for that matter.

It was a piece of wood... And it seemed a lot bigger than I initially thought. But what was this piece of wood doing so deep beneath the ground? And why did it even seem to be carved out? Why did it have such a flat surface? And why was it so rectangularly shaped?

Star looked around for the umpteenth time. She had to hurry because time was of the essence here. After all, it wouldn't be long before the light outside would go completely on darkness again. And if that were to happen, and before she had lit all the candles in their treehouse, neither she nor Grandpa Maxwell would even see a hand in front of their eyes in all that pitch-black darkness. Moreover, her grandfather wouldn't be happy with it at all. The man-human would even find it very childish of her, because only very small children would sometimes forget to burn a candle, just before the light would go completely out again. No, that wouldn't happen to Star. That hadn't happened to her for at least an era... Star had to make sure she got on the move, and fast!

Star now lies on her nest, panting, puffing, and with a pounding heart in her throat. In her hands, she holds a mysterious object that she'd just taken from the soil of the vegetable garden. This time, she didn't get the chance to cook a tasty tuber jar. On the other hand, she had managed to lit the candles in time; just before Maxwell was to return from his wandering through Alfalfa...

She had managed to repair the hole in the garden, just so that it looked as if there had never been any digging at all. However, her clothes are still dirty, and her shadow is magnified by the burning candle, thus covering most of the wooden walls around her. As if she's some big creature, a shadow giant that could escape through the open window at free will, an opening which, behind a green and also vast landscape, eagerly awaits her... For now, however, she's holding a wooden box that she looks at full of questions. She picks off the strands of braided leaves that tie the lid to the box with trembling hands. Why would Grandpa Maxwell have hidden this wooden box from her? And why so deeply beneath the ground? Could this box contain more information, memories, or objects from her parents, perhaps? Would she finally, just finally, find out more about them? Star almost wanted to lift the lid, although there was also something that stopped her from doing so. She had calmed down a bit while laying her hands on the closed wooden container, just to be able to think for a while in silence. Of course, Grandpa Maxwell hadn't just hidden this object from her for nothing, now had he? Perhaps she was still too young for this information about her parents? Maybe her grandfather wanted to wait for the reveal until she was a bit older? But Star's curiosity soon took over. Surely she was entitled to what belonged to her, to what truly concerned her? Star lifted the lid of the box very slowly, and the light of the candle took a look in the box along with her...

At the bottom of the box, there seemed to be some kind of book. Star took it out and looked at the image on the front. A circle with an oak tree inside was what seemed to adorn the front cover. At the bottom right were two letters visible that Star had accidentally managed to uncover when she tried to remove some earth and sand from the front. The two letters read: *M.B...*

She let the book rest on her lap for a moment and pricked up her ears, wondering if grandpa could come up the stairs at any moment, but the only thing she could hear was some low snoring from the floor underneath that of her own. Star quickly, but also silently, opened the book and then started reading...

She sat on her nest for almost the entire darkness, with a flaming candle next to her side, which burned calmly. But the more information the young Star seemed to take in, the more the despair grew, whether she should continue with the reading... With every sentence placed, there seemed to be a question mark rising. Nevertheless, Star just couldn't stop with the reading, because this book specifically seemed to be tailored to her; a book that specifically had been written for her…

Her heart started beating faster again, although it didn't seem to be because of a healthy tension. She also noticed how both her tongue and throat started to get dry. What kind of weird thing was this anyway? And what kind of strange game was actually being played here? Didn't grandpa know that Star liked nothing more than immersing herself in the beautiful nature which surrounds their community? Why hadn't the man given her this book much earlier? Why did this beautifully bound book contain all kinds of illustrations of trees, shrubs, plants, and also flowers that she didn't seem to recognize at all? Flora that she'd never even seen bloom and grow in Alfalfa or outside? Could it be her grandfather, maybe? Was he perhaps the unknown author of this biological work? She looked at the two letters again: *M.B... Could this be the name of the writer?*

In any case, the first letter started with an *M.*, and grandpa's name also started with this letter. Moreover, Star also knew that her grandfather was a gifted draftsman, although he hadn't done anything with it for at least an era. Was it him perhaps? Who had made these illustrations? Yet, that wasn't even the strangest thing of all. No, the strangest thing was the unknown words with which these crops were designated. Because Star recognized the sketch of the thin crooked tree all too well, but it was really the word 'palm' that was written underneath the drawing... The yellow curved fruit had 'banana' written under it. The green slime vegetable 'okra.' The fluffy plant had the word 'cotton' written underneath. And the sweet tuber was suddenly depicted as a 'yam...'

What did these words even mean? Were they their names? A forgotten language, perhaps? That consciously was kept from an underling like Star? Had her own grandfather gone much further into the forest before? And did the man have a certain middle name? A certain surname that no one ever knew about? However, Star was startled when the light from outside suddenly went on again.

She quickly put the book back in the chest, tied the strand of braided leaves tightly around both the lid and the body of the chest, and then quickly hid the object in a hidden place somewhere in her private quarters. She straightened her back, washed both herself and her clothes with some cold water, and then walked somewhat cautiously down the stairs; all the way to the ground floor. Her grandfather had apparently been up a little sooner, and he was just blowing out his own candle when he saw his granddaughter descending the spiral stairs...

'Have a good revolution, Star! Did you sleep well...?'

But when Maxwell took a closer look at his granddaughter, he could also see that something wasn't quite right.

'What's wrong, Star? Haven't you been able to sleep well? You look so tired still. You even have bags under your eyes. I've never noticed those on you...'

Star didn't know what to say, of course. She had indeed read through the entire darkness and hadn't slept a wink. But should she tell this man the truth? Or keep this secret to herself? She rubbed her eyes a little longer than usual, which gave her a small moment to quickly come to a decision. But Star also knew that by now, through the many cycles that laid behind her, she already had quite a few secrets to her name. And even though these could be counted on only one hand, they were at least four fingers thick. And if she were to reveal this secret, she should do the same with the other ones. But would that actually benefit her? Would this man be open to such revelations? Was this man actually who he said he was? And could this man actually be trusted? Star decided to come up with an excuse and said that the beginning of this cycle, and especially the learning-bench, had been tough on her. Her schedule is already so full, and she simply couldn't sleep in the previous darkness because she was worrying about whether she would be able to handle it all in the near future... But the old man, now standing next to her, suddenly had to laugh out loud.

'But, dear Star... The cycle has only just begun. Don't get ahead of yourself like that. Just take it as it comes. Keep putting in the effort as you have so far, and everything will be fine. You'll get there eventually. I don't think you want to stay a novice forever, now do you? Here's a nice tuber for you...'

And the man takes out a wooden plate with two edible boiled tubers on it. Star's heart seemed to skip a beat, and she looked at her grandfather somewhat anxiously. The man then puts his hand on her shoulder, exactly as one of the elders had done to her recently, while he looks at her just as seriously.

'What's wrong with you, Star? Acting all cramped up? This here is the edible tuber of the woody shrub. It's one of your favorites, isn't it? You've always loved that one, haven't you?' Star took a deep breath and then nodded.

'I do like that one, Grandpa. I'm sorry. I've been quite tense in the past revolutions...'

'I know, sweetheart,' is what her grandfather encouragingly says to her as he playfully pats her on the head. 'I had already noticed that in you. And that's why I have a surprise for you this revolution!' And the man walked away for a moment, after which he came back with some reed stems...

Star joyfully jumped into the air; somewhat theatrically, and played. 'Sugar cane! One of my favorites!' Grandpa gave her a kiss on the cheek. 'They're all for you, but don't use them up in one go, okay?'

Star nodded affably for the umpteenth time. She followed the slow footsteps of Grandpa Maxwell with suspicion, nevertheless, which led him through their spiral treehouse and towards their shared vegetable garden...

With a Spear at the Ready

Not far before the first checkpoint, at post number sixty-six over the fence, and then about five hundred steps straight ahead... Would the forest wanderer still live there? And what would it actually look like? Would it have a monstrous appearance? And would it actually be able to talk? Or would it want to devour Star because it hadn't eaten for so long and because it's hungry?

'You're crazy for doing this, Star,' is what she says to herself as she stands at the numbered post; the post of the right fence, which runs parallel to the narrow gravel path that she's been walking on for a while now.

She looks a bit further on the gravel path. The path continues for a long stretch and then seems to make a left turn in the distance. If she's to believe the stories of the underlings, this path reaches all the way to the Betanex community; the community where the new male-boy in her learning-bench apparently comes from. A community that Star had never visited before. But Star had never visited another community anyway. No, she actually only knows Alfalfa. Her world is but small. Moreover, one has to pass a checkpoint full of guards if one wants to visit Betanex, for example. And one had to get a certificate of approval for that, followed by permission to travel... Star looks behind her for a moment, no guard in sight, it seems...

You're crazy for doing this, Star... is the only thing she can think of when she looks at post number sixty-six, jumps over the fence, and then disappears into the bushes as silently as possible...

When Star arrives at the cave, she doesn't really know what to do, or how to behave. She has only been here once before, and that was quite some time ago. Once before, during her super forbidden trips through the forest; looking for some rampant growing crops that she may not have known yet, and from which she might learn some more. Star gently touches the pendant that lies under her vest and rests on her sternum. She also feels the book that she'd just opened for the very first time during the previous darkness, and that she now has hidden behind her back between her trousers waist and vest. A book that had persuaded her to be here again; here in front of the lair of the dangerous forest wanderer…

She has taken a homemade wooden spear with her, just in case she's being attacked by this monster. And in her other palm, she holds an eye-stinging powder that she possibly could blow into his eyes if things would really go wrong, and if this forest creature wanted to kidnap her and let her wander around in the forest forever, just like itself did.

Star will have to have her pressing questions answered. And if all should go wrong, and should the wanderer cut her down in an attack, then at least she would have done her best, and she would've followed her heart.

And according to her, at least, that was still worth more than the biggest chunk of fool's gold she could ever find... With the wooden spear and eye-stinging powder firmly in hand, and prepared for everything that might come her way, she calls into the cave...

'Is anyone there?! Wanderer?! Anyone?! Are you there?!' But it remained deadly quiet. Even quieter than a moment before. And it was almost as if the trees outside were listening, the teeming animals and insects had crawled back into their burrows, and the birds had stopped whistling their tunes for a moment...

Nevertheless, something happened that Star hadn't expected beforehand; something that made her lower her wooden spear somewhat while pointing its carved-out out sharp ending a bit more towards the ground. Nonetheless, she held the stinging powder even firmer. It could of course also be a trap...

A muffled, but also friendly voice, spoke to her, somewhere from the back of the cave: 'Please, do come in, whoever you are. I have nothing to hide. And if you are one of the guards, you should know that fact by now, and I really don't understand what you are doing here in the first place...'

Star walked through the dark, narrow tunnel of the cave, and at the end of it shone a warm and friendly light. When she arrived there, she saw an elderly woman bent over on a wooden seat. The woman held a feather in her hand and seemed to dip it in some black liquid that laid on a small ceramic plate. The somewhat older woman just looked up when Star stepped out of the darkness.

'Guard... What brings you here this revolution?' But the elderly woman dropped her feather in fright when she saw that it wasn't some guard entering her cave dwelling, but a female cub.

'Damn it!' was what she exclaimed. 'Who are you?! What brings you here?!'

But Star aimed the sharp spearhead bravely towards the woman.

'Don't approach me!' she shouted loudly. 'Don't attack me!' And so the two stood opposite each other for a little while. Not really knowing who it was they were dealing with exactly, and not knowing who the real threat exactly was here.

Star decided to speak first. She was the one who had entered this domain on her own accord, and the resident had therefore some right to an explanation.

'I'm looking for the forest wanderer! She shouted. Where is he?! And when will he come back?! I'm willing to use this spear if I have to!' But the older woman laughed just as loudly at these bold statements, and she calmly picked up her writing quill again. 'It is you who had the audacity to enter my domain,' was what the woman said. 'So it seems clear to me that you first tell me who you are, where it is you are coming from, and what your motivation precisely is to be here... Alfalfa, you say? Hmm. And your name is Star? Never heard of it... But do lower your spear, young female-girl, and listen to what I have to say to you...' And that was exactly what Star did. She lowered her homemade weapon and listened to what the woman had to say to her...

'Don't be alarmed, Star, but it looks like you've found the right person. It is indeed I. I am the one they call the forest wanderer...'

'You can't mean that...' Star said in surprise. 'You don't look dangerous or monstrous at all...'

'No, that's right," said the woman. 'I'm just an ordinary woman-human who likes to be on her own. But do tell me, what's the real reason why you're here? What motivation has brought you to me, and to my dwelling?'

Star calmly walked towards the woman, at the same time took the book from behind her trouser waist, and then opened it on the wooden worktop on which the woman had worked so furiously a few moments ago. The woman squinted her eyes into two narrow stripes and then read the random pages that had just been opened in front of her. 'So… that's interesting…' was what she calmly said. 'I haven't experienced something so exciting and exhilarating in a long time. Thanks, Star…' But the woman didn't say much more about it for the rest. 'Is that all you have to say to this?!' was what Star somewhat angrily asked.

'Don't you understand what this could implicate? Don't you understand that these crops could be much further and deeper within the forest?'

But the woman looked at Star with exasperation. 'Of course I understand that, cub! But what am I about to do with this all? What do you want me to do with this exactly?' 'Well…' said Star in a controlled manner. 'Perhaps you can tell me more about this information? Where this greenery can be found, for example. And why do we, as citizens, know nothing about them at all?'

'Hmm..' was what the elderly woman said again, and she scratched her nose for a moment. 'Maybe I can tell you more about this matter, but perhaps also not.'

She closed the book again and gave it back to her unexpected guest. Nevertheless, this was anything but what Star had hoped for, and she had no intention of leaving this place until she found out more about this.

'Maybe? You say? Maybe?!' was what she repeated in frustration. 'They don't call you the forest wanderer for nothing, do they? I mean to say...

You always travel and wander through the forest alone, don't you? That's your method, isn't it? But the woman shook her head in a controlled manner and tapped a few times with her quill on a piece of parchment that had taken the place of Star's book again.

'They only call me the forest wanderer because it's claimed that I confuse people seemingly, and that I let them wander in the surrounding bushes for eternity...'

'But who claims that?' asked Star curiously.

'Who do you think, Star?!' The woman said with a stern face. The people, of course, the underlings within the communities, you must know that by now, don't you?!' Star nodded, although she initially had expected a different outcome, the elders perhaps...?

'But that story has to come from somewhere, right?' was what she asked.

'Yes,' the woman said. 'It has been brought into this world deliberately...'

'Made up?' asked Star again in surprise. 'But by whom? And for what purpose?'

'Well, by whom, do you think?!' the woman exclaimed again, now irritated.

'By the elders, of course!' Star was shocked by what the woman suddenly made known to her. The elders...

so her suspicions were true after all...

Yet, Star wisely decided not to ask any further questions, because it might put her in a certain spotlight too much, if that wasn't the case already...

'But before you start asking me more of your tiring questions, questions that I probably don't know the answers to, to begin with, I advise you to consult the statue of immeasurable wisdom... And maybe, just maybe, it will show you the way to the hall of forgotten knowledge... Perhaps there you will find more clues about the origin of all those mysterious plant species from your book. I myself have been consulting the statue for many cycles, and if you really are chosen, if you're really worthy, it even seems to speak back at you, although it has never exchanged a word with me, unfortunately... Unfortunately, I have never been granted access to this hall of knowledge. All that I'm really looking for is some peace and inner reflection, because as you've already seen, I don't have anyone else to talk to here...'

'And where exactly can I find that statue?' was what Star asked, somewhat delighted that this visit to the forest wanderer went so peacefully, and that she, at any moment now, might even get a clue that could possibly continue her search.

The woman pointed into the distance, towards a location that could be anywhere since the two were currently in a closed space.

'It's a long way in that direction,' the woman said. 'Far beyond the first checkpoint. A long way beyond the narrow gravel path that you undoubtedly know.'

'I don't know...' said Star suspiciously. 'Perhaps you are trying to get me lost...' But the woman sniffed her nose contemptuously.

'Believe what you want, female-child, but your search has brought you to this cave for a reason. I also used to have my questions, my doubts, because we seem to live in a world where there are more open questions than answered suspicions... But I'm done talking to you. And if your curiosity has won over your fear in the coming revolutions, there will be a drawn road map that will point you to the hall of knowledge, laying outside in front of this cave under a large stone, the next time you visit here again. I don't give it to you just yet, because I want you to think about this very thoroughly back at home. Back in Alfalfa, wasn't it? So, think carefully about what your next steps will be. Do you leave everything for what it is? Or are you willing to look beyond the end of your own suspicions? This choice is entirely up to you... But please, leave me alone for now. And if you are here the next time, don't come in, and don't knock on my walls with any of your weaponry, because I won't be here. And if I am here, I will pretend not to be, because I will be hiding from you... I have seen enough for this cycle already with all this. Go now!'

Star sits back on her nest in that darkness, with a straight candle flame next to her side. She couldn't really think of anything else than the words of the 'forest wanderer.' Of the opportunity she had offered Star. And of the inner fight that the woman seemed to realize all too well, and that Star was now worrying about... That inner battle between fear and curiosity. Because Star was wise enough to know that fear could be a protective thing, but at the same time also could have a paralyzing effect. Curiosity, on the other hand, could be an impulsive thing; it could cause her problems, but could also lead to new and profound discoveries... What could this choice bring her? What would the alleged drawn roadmap contribute to her own life? Could it be nothing more than problems? Or perhaps a discovery that could change her little world forever...?

Tricky Questions…

Something unexpected happened during the next revolution. The learning-bench had been over for a while, and on the way to her spiral home, Star was being chased. When she turned around, her pursuer turned out to be none other than the new man-boy: Thomias… The boy had been following her all along, apparently, but what had he to do with her? The boy looked at her for a moment, looked away again, but then decided to walk up to Star to introduce himself nicely. The male-boy held out his hand and then said the following: 'Hi, I'm Thomias.'

But Star couldn't contain her laughter, and so she laughed out loud. This was perhaps the driest thing she had experienced lately; just the way he said it alone.

'Are you laughing at me or something?' was what the boy asked in surprise.

'No,' said Star in all honesty. 'I just had to laugh a little at the way you introduced yourself. I mean, I already know your name, don't I?'

Thomias nodded. 'That's true, but I don't really know yours yet, now do I?

And I thought I'd neatly introduce myself first. At least, that's how we were taught in Betanex, but perhaps that custom is different here? I really don't know…' But now it was Thomias who had to laugh for a moment. 'Jeez, Star, I'm just trying to do something here…' But the boy suddenly put a hand over his mouth, somewhat startled.

'Ha!' said Star. 'So you do know my name!'

'Yes,' said Thomias, with a slight blush on his cheeks. 'I mean, I said: I don't really know your name yet. I just wanted to hear it from your mouth. Gosh, Star, don't you want to talk to me or something? Because that's the impression I'm getting a bit now. I find it a difficult conversation already...' Star briefly touched the pendant that rested under her cardigan.

'Well,' she said. 'I'm not really sure what it is you want to talk about...?'

'Well!' said Thomias, suddenly and loudly. 'We could talk about anything, right? I mean, you had already caught my eye, Star. You just seem like a female-girl who has something to say. Not like all those other stiff ones among those underlings...' Star looked at him nicely for a moment. This was indeed a compliment out of an unexpected corner, and on top of that, a completely unconventional one also. Perhaps she could say more to this man-boy, to this Thomias, than she'd initially thought?

'I'd really like to talk to you more often, Thomias, but...' And Star thought for a moment whether she should say this or not. 'I'm just not sure what it is I can tell you, and what not...' But instead of being frightened or somewhat dismayed, a small and mysterious grimace appeared on Thomias' face.

'I also carry some kind of secret with me, Star,' was what he suddenly said. 'Something I'd really like to share with you, but I also don't know if you're open to...'

Star looked mesmerized at the boy for a moment, before he could even finish his sentence. Where did all this come from all of a sudden? Wasn't she the only 'rebellious one' within the community of Alfalfa after all?

'I'm open to more things than you might suspect at first glance,' was what she very maturely and also very politically correct said.

'Good!' said Thomias, delighted all of a sudden. 'Then let's make each other a promise. If I tell you a secret of mine first, then you have to reveal something of yourself to me afterwards, okay?' Star touched the contours of her necklace pendant again for a moment, although talking about it might be something she would have to wait a bit longer for. Nevertheless, Star also nodded happily with this agreement. 'Agreed!' was therefore what she said. And the two sealed their mutual vow with a friendly handshake.

The many revolutions that followed were mainly spent together by Thomias and Star. Their mutual trust grew significantly with time, and so they knew more and more about each other. They now both knew from each other that they both aspired to a forbidden passion. Star, of course, had her striving for a knowledge of plants, of their components, and of their almost magical effects, while Thomias, on the other hand, was concerned with quite different matters. The male-boy seemed to have developed a taste for something he himself labeled as 'technology'. A word he had in his head for many cycles but didn't even know what it actually meant... Star hadn't told him anything about the hanger dangling around her neck yet, nor about the book she had found in her vegetable garden.

However, she had told him about her occasional trips deeper into the forest; something which seemed to surprise the boy, and which also seemed to arouse his own curiosity somewhat. Nevertheless, Star thought that this tossed-up ball was all up to Thomias, even though she couldn't wait for the revolution that he would ask her more about it. And even though she didn't really want to drag him into all this, at the same time, she couldn't get the roadmap out of her head that the forest wanderer had laid out for her somewhere under a large stone in front of her cave. Because, would that map actually be there? And would she dare to take that step on her own? Or would someone like Thomias perhaps want to go with her to find out more about all this? Star fervently hoped for the latter, of course. How could she ask him this calmly without forcing herself onto him?

However, at one of the revolutions, already almost in the middle of the cycle, she seemed to have found an opening for this. She decided to just ask him. She hadn't had that much to lose. And soon the roadmap might have already been snatched away by someone else; taken away by some other rebellious soul. And that could have been done by anyone; by any other underling with a 'curious disposition,' as one of the elders once titled her. And that specific underling could come from the Betanex, from Gammanon, from Deltarion, or perhaps even from the distant Epsilonia... The two sat together again at another revolution; somewhere just outside Alfalfa, right under the tall trees amidst their lianas. Star began to understand and remember the 'forbidden concepts' from her book better and better, although she also knew that she couldn't discuss them with her good friend Thomias yet. She nevertheless discussed almost everything with him, including her increasingly suffocating relationship with her grandfather, Maxwell. Star also knew that she'd always been fairly good to her grandpa, and he, of course, was also good to her, but there always seemed to be a certain distance in between them, and Star thought she understood better now why that was exactly. She hadn't taken the man all too seriously in the past, but with today's knowledge, that seemed even more the case. She never showed it in an overt way so that it would hurt the man, but she did show it more and more frequently lately, and her grandfather had to feel this under his skin also. However, it was something that was never talked about, and they both acted as if there was no friction between them at all. Yet, this mutual tension was increasingly felt within their shared treehouse. As if these clashing energies began to accumulate more and more in their wooden spiral home. As if these vibrations were less and less able to find a way out; not through Star's open bedroom window, also not through the open vault of their large hollow treehouse, actually through nowhere anymore...

'It's quite strange actually...' was what Thomias said to Star on another revolution. 'It's quite strange that the elders said that everyone should let me get used to the infrastructure here in Alfalfa. I mean... It looks exactly like ours in Betanex, only the location is slightly different...' However, Star decided not to just accept this as a common fact. The elders seemed to say a lot lately, and she believed less and less what was coming out of their mouths, in any case. Instead, she spouts her own displeasure about Grandpa Maxwell. Perhaps

Thomias has something meaningful to say about that? She tells him that she just can't understand why Grandpa Maxwell remains so stuck in his rigidity. As if this is all there is. As if Alfalfa is the summum and there are no other truths besides it. The good man seems to be fine with it all, and Star says to Thomias that she's less and less able to cope with it anymore. Why does she have to learn from people like him? People who supposedly know how life works? Without any chance to argue against it? Even though Star sees things so differently so often? Why isn't the man a bit more rebellious? Why is he so... so... timid and close-minded...?!

'Well...' says Thomias. 'He is a man-person at an advanced age, of course.

I don't find it that strange at all that he is so timid. What do you want him to do? Some form of crazy dance? Jumping up and down wildly? Soon, the good man might fall apart by doing so...' But Star couldn't laugh at this at all. 'But he's always been like that...' is what she says when she looks towards the location of their spiral treehouse. 'He has never been adventurous. He has never deviated from the beaten path. He has always, and only, stayed in line to comply with the rules of Alfalfa as well as possible. Because that's just the way it is. That's the only and real truth!'

'Shh,' hissed Thomias angrily. 'Don't talk so loudly, soon they will hear you... I mean... Us...' But Star looked away in annoyance for a moment. 'Yes, you're also such a hero in socks. I'm almost starting to think that all man-people are like that...' But Thomias couldn't let this go his way, of course. 'Well...' he said dubiously. 'I may be somewhat of a quiet guy, but I also regularly doubt the state of affairs within the communities. But hey! What can you do about it? And I'm not going to... I'm certainly not going to shout that from the treetops like you do. Only dumb and naïve people express their opinions so openly...'

But the boy got a color on his cheeks after saying this, and perhaps the words were a bit too sharply placed. 'Sorry...' was what he quickly said. 'Perhaps I shouldn't have said that...' But instead of getting angry or feeling hurt in her honor, Star lowered her head, somewhat defeated. 'No... I'm afraid you are absolutely right. It appears that I will never be allowed to fully and openly express my heart. And I even think that that's where the curse of my life lies. Because life is definitely beautiful...' And Star extended her arm for a moment, moving it sideways to indicate all the lush greenery around her. '...But what really lies close to my heart, I just can't seem to reach. It seems very likely that I too will have to join the crowd; a crowd that doesn't seem to know any better, and which allows itself to be completely overshadowed by the collective...'

'Maybe you're right...' said Thomias somewhat sadly, but at the same time in a sympathetic way. 'Maybe that's just the case. Perhaps the group is indeed stronger than the individual. And perhaps that's why it's so damn difficult to try and enforce any change within that collective. No matter how big or small the change might be. And no matter in which community out there...'

'Yes, I think you're absolutely right,' said Star finally. 'I'm probably just naïve, while letting my feelings determine my actions too much...'

Thomias picked up a random pebble and wanted to hit a tree with it, but missed and hit some bushes instead. 'There's nothing wrong with that in itself, Star, ' was what he said. 'But you know... Perhaps your grandfather was a rebel too, once in his lifetime? The man has been around for many eras. What do you know of how much his old eyes have seen? Perhaps he's seen much more than you and I can imagine? And maybe he has decided for himself that this is the best way to live the last part of his life? This life, and the many cycles, and the countless revolutions, that he has been spending with you...?'

'I don't think so!' exclaimed Star suddenly bitterly, and an awkward silence followed. A silence from which Thomias could make out more than his already good friend wanted to tell him. And Star decided to tell him her deepest secrets, including the inner plan that seemed to grow with every revolution; the plan to look for the hall of forgotten knowledge; a place that the forest wanderer had told her about a while ago...

Thomias didn't really knew what he'd gotten himself into. From the very first moment when he'd seen Star, he had acquired a certain fascination for her. From that very first impression, he could conclude that there was something special about this female youngster from Alfalfa. Nevertheless, this here was more adventure than he had hoped for. Thomias also had something like relatives; other underlings close to him, who had come to live with him in this community, and he also had a certain responsibility towards them, of course. Who was this adventurous female-girl? This fascinating creature that he was now hobbling behind? As tamely as a meek lamb? Was he actually doing the right thing with this? Wouldn't it be much better for him to turn around? In order to lead a quiet life, just like the other underlings did? Immerse himself completely in his chosen industry of working with building materials? An industry in which he could reasonably practice with his self-invented term? With his self-made-up word? That which he described as 'technology'? Star's enthusiasm seemed to have a certain attraction to him. And it was something that he just couldn't seem to resist. Yet, he couldn't deny that he carried a certain fear within. And he let it shine through to Star when they'd arrived at the place they'd been looking for, for quite some time now...

The two had taken the wanderer's map from under the stone in front of her lair, and they had been following the trail that could be read from this piece of parchment for a long time now. But Star had also thought carefully for a moment, while she heard the creaking twigs behind her that Thomias trampled under his feet during their walk. Was that perhaps what the forest wanderer was doing all this time? Writing down roadmaps for any underling that had his or her questions? It almost had to be... And Star simultaneously looked at the road map she was holding in her hands. This can't be the only copy...

The ink with which the words were written, and the route with which it was drawn, was far too legible for that. The forest wanderer also seemed a creature who knew much more than she initially wanted to tell, and she also seemed to keep her mouth shut. Was that perhaps an unwritten rule within this world? One was allowed to have secrets within the communities, but one was absolutely not allowed to talk about them openly?

Star didn't understand that at all... Well, she understood it, but she didn't comprehend it at the same time. Because, why? Why would anyone choose secrecy over honesty? Why would anyone want to live like this? All secluded and hidden? And Thomias, too, seemed to be cut from the same cloth. He also didn't like to carry secrets along with him. Also, not due to this newly emerged adventure, which, according to him, would irrevocably result in unpleasant consequences. He was already done with it at this point. And he let Star know this very clearly. He was already feeling anxious a moment ago, but this feeling only seemed to increase; with every step with which he chased Star, and with every twig that snapped under his well-placed feet... Thomias looked a bit pale, and he looked at Star somewhat panicky:

'Star...' he said. 'I really don't know if we're doing the right thing here... Perhaps we should go back...'

But Star wouldn't think of it. She felt no fear at all actually, and this double life that she seemed to lead for quite some time now, actually began to grow more and more on her. 'Not a hair on my head, Thomias,' was what she said.

'We have already come so far. I even think we are in the right place.

We are just going to take a quick look and then go back right before darkness sets in. Nothing is the matter here...'

Thomias wiped some cold sweat from his forehead and started to feel a bit lightheaded. 'But Star... This is simply too dangerous. Even... even for someone like you!' Thomias actually wanted to say 'us', but he had never experienced this kind of thing before, and for him, this was the most dangerous and the most precarious thing he had ever undertaken so far. Nevertheless, he didn't want to profile himself as a coward either. He was still the man-boy here, and if anyone needed protection, it was Star, and certainly not him!

Thomias decided to stay for a while, even though he felt like he could empty his stomach at any moment now; somewhere there in between the lush greenery...

'Hmm,' said Star. 'It must be here somewhere.' And she looked at the piece of parchment that she was holding in her hands. 'Yes, this really has to be the place...' She scraped some moss off an unusual-looking surface with the wooden spearhead, and a part of a flat, decorated stone suddenly appeared.

'Say, Thomias, what kind of special thing is this?' But when Star tried to take a closer look at the strangely decorated stone, both she and Thomias heard a voice that seemed to come from a little further away. The two looked at each other for a moment and then carefully walked around the completely moss-covered mound. There, half hidden under the greenery, draped by a number of brownish lianas, appeared a large stone monster that already stood waiting for them with its big gaping mouth. It looked like they had found the statue! The hall of forgotten knowledge couldn't be too far away by now!

Thomias walked with trembling knees behind Star, who bravely walked towards the large statue with the wooden spear at the ready. Thomias could beat himself up for it. Who actually needed protection here, anyway?

A hero in socks was indeed what he was, and he kept watching from a safe distance as Star tried to speak to the fear-inducing image. But this statue seemed anything but to tolerate the bravery of an ordinary underling. The stone statue had the first word here and Star, and the observing Thomias, would know that very soon. A low roaring voice sounded from the mouth of the stone beast: 'Who has the guts to consult me in this place?! Who are you, little lady-woman?! And how do you know of my presence here?!'

Star mentioned her name, and also that of Thomias, and she also told the true reason for their visit.

'So, you bold mortals seek a passing to the hall of forgotten knowledge?!'

There lingered an icy silence in the air for a moment, although to her surprise, Star also had to laugh to herself a bit. Because, in her own mind, she saw this large stone statue scratching itself behind the ear already, while it was so busy doing its thinking. She wasn't afraid of it at all, actually. She didn't feel any fear. And somewhere deep inside, she thought the reason why...

'The hall of forgotten knowledge...' the statue suddenly said pedantically. 'How does someone like you know of such?'

And Star told about her meeting with the forest wanderer. About the map that had been drawn out for her. And how it had brought them both to this wondrous place; here in front of the big gaping mouth of this stone monster...

'The forest wanderer...?' asked the statue

rhetorically to itself.

'That explains a lot... She must have seen something in you... Something that makes us come out of our nest at the beginning of a new revolution, just after the light goes on... Ehm, I mean you guys... What you sort makes you come out of your nests at the beginning of a new revolution...'

It was quiet again for a while, and Star could hardly suppress a smile.

'To the point!' was what the stone statue suddenly exclaimed. 'I can't just grant you passage for nothing. This here is the sanctuary of the nature spirits, and they will therefore have to be reassured. They simply contribute great value to knowledge and wisdom...'

Thomias had also joined in the meantime, at the same time, not knowing how to behave exactly, although the statue didn't confer too much value to his presence. Of course, it was mainly Star's presence that seemed to excite this large statue. That Star... She even seemed capable of softening the heart of a stone monster...

'...And therefore you two will have to redeem worthy!' continued the statue's low roaring voice. 'I will grant you three questions... Three questions that will have to be solved altogether within a tenth of a revolution. And I will continue to wait for you here; curious about the solutions you two will grant me. Besides, it doesn't look like I'm going anywhere else in the meantime, now does it...'

Thomias suddenly had to laugh aloud, after which he quickly held a hand over his mouth in fright again.

Perhaps it was his nerves that had to come out this way. Perhaps, because he was slightly relieved that this statue didn't seem to mean any harm. Although he didn't want to evoke the wrath of this monstrous statue with his uncontrolled laughter. He wisely decided to keep his mouth shut. In any case, he could feel the eyes of this statue painfully stinging on his face...

'If you fail to solve these questions within the given timeframe, or if you get one of them wrong, you will curse yourself forever, and this will be the last revolution you will be spending in this forest. For the forest spirits will come to take you into the coming darkness, and they will drag you down into their underground world, so that you can be used there as malicious pleasure during their playfully wicked games. Not such a bright prospect, I thought so, hmm? So, think carefully and decide wisely. What do you say? Yay or Nay?'

Star looked at Thomias mockingly for a moment, while Thomias in turn looked at her with some tightness in his eyes. Star still had that mysterious grin on her face. Thomias, on the other hand; the man of technology and self-proclaimed inventor of—basically nothing yet to show for—wanted nothing more than to leave, and right about now! To leave this stupid image for what it was. That was the only thing he could think of right now. They had to go! And so immediately! This image wouldn't be able to catch up with them anyway.

And if they were to leave now, this monster might have forgotten about them in the next revolution. Let another fool become a forest wanderer.

Let some other underling become a plaything of the

nature spirits, whoever or whatever they may be. This is too dangerous!

'Yes, of course,' said Star dryly. 'We'll accept your offer. We'll take the challenge.'

'You have decided!' was what the statue satisfied said. 'Brace yourselves for the first question!'

'What??!!' was what Thomias blared in Star's ear. 'Have you gone completely mental now??!! Are you a madwoman or something?! Helloooooo! I'm standing right here you know. I'm still around too, you know! You are crazy!

I should've never come along with you!' But Star said, in a somewhat unreasonable way, that it really had been his own choice to come along with her. She'd never forced him into doing anything at all. Moreover, he had to tone down his voice a bit, or did he want them to be caught in the act?!

Thomias could've pulled his hair out of his head by now. Woman-people! They seemed to be able to get everything done; even bending the truth so that a man-boy began to believe in it himself. *Ahh,* thought Thomas also. *It doesn't matter anyway. All was lost anyway...* And running away on his own no longer made sense now, because then he could expect unwelcome visitors during that darkness, knocking on his doorstep, while laying all alone in his nest. *Let that question come,* was what he finally thought. There is no turning back now anyways. But he didn't like this little joke of Star for one bit. No, he couldn't appreciate it at all...

'Brace yourselves, brave, but also foolish underlings. Here are all of your questions... Question number one:

What is the anomaly of water...?

Question number two: *Who is the greatest artist who always is, always has been, and always will be...?*

And finally, and also the last question, and also one of my favorites: *Which human aspect is both his greatest curse, as well as his greatest blessing...?*

But Thomias suddenly felt nauseous again, and he wanted to disappear into the bushes further on again for a while. Not to flee of course, because it was already too late for that. No, just to see what he had eaten at the very start of this revolution... He had always considered himself reasonably intelligent and smart, but these were questions that went far over his head. How could they ever bring this to a successful conclusion? Star seemed to be able to read the hopelessness of his face, and she too, was shocked by the difficulty of these questions. But what if they just sat down quietly for a while? Surely they could get one or two questions right, right? They had to win the respect of this statue, whatever the cost may be.

'I'm sure it will be okay, Thomias,' was what she reassuringly said to her buddy.

'But gosh, what difficult questions. I don't even know what... anomaly was it...? Even means...' And so they sat on the surrounding lush grass for a while. And the more they thought about these questions, the more potential answers forced themselves onto them. Perhaps it was the natural beauty that gave them this inspiration. Perhaps, because they had nowhere to go anyway, or the pressure of the urgent time frame, but in any case, they quickly found a trail that Thomias, in particular, fiercely elaborated on.

'Well... anomaly...' said Thomias to himself questioningly. 'I don't really know the word either. But yeah... If you put it in the context of the sentence, it might be something like 'strange?' Or 'special?' So maybe it's something like: What's so strange or special about water? What aspect? And while Thomias was thinking about that matter, Star mused about the second question and thought she might even have found a suitable answer to it. Now only the third question remained...

What human aspect is both his greatest curse as well as his greatest blessing? Both of them had now, silently and without knowing it from each other, arrived at this question. And Star had to think for a moment about her earlier conversation with the forest wanderer: about the inner struggle between fear and curiosity... But when she tried to suggest this fact to Thomias, he already seemed one step ahead of her. As if they both, and without knowing it from each other, possessed the same speed in terms of train of thought. As if they were on the same wavelength, whatever that might mean...

'Jeez, Star,' said Thomias again. 'Personally, I find the last question very difficult. I really have no idea...' But without Thomias fully realizing it, the answer already seemed hidden in this questioned statement, and Star seemed to realize this given.

'I think I already know the answer Thomias,' she said.

'It has to be our own train of thought. It can hardly be otherwise. Let's consult the statue again. We really need to be home before darkness kicks in...'

Thomias couldn't agree more with this, and with

their findings in mind, they walked towards the large stone statue that seemed to stare so quietly into nothingness...

Star, cheeky as she was, was of course the first to walk towards the stone beast...

'Statue!' she pompously stated. 'We think we know the answers.'

'Okay,' said the image. 'And that within the agreed time-frame. I have to hand it to you two... And I assume you have deliberated?' Star looked at Thomias for a moment and shook her head, and Thomias did the same. 'Well... Perhaps somewhat...' said Star doubtfully.

'That's the first stitch you've dropped,' said the stone beast. 'This is anything but wise of you...' But Star gradually got a pointed head from that word, and she wished that this stone statue would just shut up for once and would just listen to them. 'Okay, I'm listening,' said the monstrous statue, as if it could hear Star's thoughts.

'I'm the one that starts!' shouted Thomias all of a sudden.

Because he had the feeling that Star wouldn't get this question right anyway.

At least, not in the way he had thought about it.

'I think...' said the man-boy from Betanex. 'I think that the strange thing about water is... is that it doesn't actually have its own shape, but that it can take on any particular shape if you'd pour it into that form...'

And he looked proudly at Star for a moment. 'Yes! Right, Star? Think, for example, of some water in a stone pot. It really takes the shape of the pot itself, now doesn't it?' Star was indeed impressed, and the statue was also quiet for a moment.

'Good,' said the image. In a tone, Thomias couldn't make out whether he got the question right or whether the stone beast just wanted to continue. But probably the latter. Because... 'The second question!' was what the statue soon expressed.

Star now began to doubt whether her answer was the right one, and not too obvious. She had related this question to her own little world, of course.

And of course she couldn't do so otherwise. After all, she didn't know any better... 'I believe...' she said pensively, 'that the greatest artist who always is, always has been, and always will be, is nature itself. Because, nature produces beautiful art, it appears and goes when it wants, and it probably will always be here with us...' Star was suddenly a lot more impressed by her answer, especially because of the way it had left her mouth. And Thomias, who was standing next to her, couldn't help but give her a physical pat on the shoulder.

'Good,' the statue mysteriously said again. 'Question number three! And probably the most difficult question of all...'

But Star had already given Thomias sort of an answer to this question a short while ago, and Thomias had, of course, managed to remember this.

'The answer to question number three must be one's own thoughts,' said Star very seriously. 'I mean...' and she assumed that the statue expected a certain explanation from her. 'They can be a curse or a blessing at the same time. They can influence someone in a positive way or work against someone...'

Thomias nodded in agreement, and the statue seemed to be dumbfounded again. They had done quite well, they thought, and the statue seemed to confirm this.

'Good...' said the statue for the third time. 'I will grant you passage to the hall. Treat the treasures you'll see with certain tact, and perhaps until someday... Perhaps until another time...'

'Darn it!' exclaimed Thomias all of a sudden. 'It scammed us! It didn't say where we can find this hall at all!' But Star thought she already had an idea, and she decided to play this 'game' a little further...

'Thomias... think about it...' she said. 'Look closely. It's a sitting monster, and monsters like these usually have to scare something off, now don't they?

Does it stand there to keep something out? And since it's sitting here like that, with this certain attitude and posture, it's probably guarding something. I bet that the hall must be behind this statue...' Star often sailed on her intuition, and of course, she was also right in this regard. After a quick search, they had found the entrance to the hall...

Finding a Way Out

The two entered a musty and dark hole, and Star used a piece of fool's gold and a piece of flint to illuminate this space in short fractions. The two couldn't believe what they saw... Books, scrolls, and many parchments emerged from the darkness and then disappeared into the darkness again. And they themselves also stood in the light for a moment and then disappeared into the darkness again. Star quickly ran outside to find a good piece of moss and then came back with an improvised, fabricated torch.

'Wow,' exclaimed Thomias somewhat childishly, but also full of admiration when Star stood next to him with the large, flickering torch in her hand.

'Can you believe this stuff?!' Thomias quickly removed some cobwebs here and there and then began to read greedily. Star, on the other hand, seemed less impressed. Of course, she was also somewhat shocked, but she couldn't deny that she hadn't expected something like this. The shock was therefore not because of the many books that laid scattered around in this space, but more because of this place; because of the location these objects laid in...

'Look at this, Star! And what about this here?!' Thomias walked wildly back and forth, not quite knowing where to start, and the poor boy seemed to have contracted a certain gold fever by now, only then in the form of knowledge-seeking.

'What kind of information is all this?!' he asked again. 'I don't understand half of it!' But just when Star wanted to look into a damaged book, she thought she heard something shuffling outside...

'Shh,' she hissed towards Thomias, while indicating with a hand movement that they both had to duck down, and that immediately! Star quickly kicked out the torch, and with bated breath, they listened to the voices of men who had to be somewhere outside and near the stone statue.

'I swear to you commander,' said a muffled voice. 'I dare to swear that I heard a voice just now, could it have been the statue that had spoken?'

But a lower, nevertheless louder voice, spoke somewhat admonishingly to this man: 'It must have been the forest wanderer,' was what this deeper voice said. 'It comes here almost every revolution. You know that by now, don't you? We have to keep moving! We don't have time for this nonsense. Also, not to take a look in there...'

And Star saw how the man looked into the hall through the gaping mouth of the stone beast. Star looked the man straight in the eye, even though she and Thomias stood completely in the dark, and this man, who apparently was called the commander, couldn't possibly notice them in this way. And even though the torch had been kicked out for a while, it was still getting a bit too hot under their feet, and especially that of Star's...

The next revolution, Thomias was especially overjoyed to be back in Alfalfa in one piece, and that without anyone noticing anything.

'It wasn't that bad, now was it?' was what Star said in a triumphant tone when she approached him; planning to get straight to the point.

'We have to find a way to get out of here,' was what she immediately added. But Thomias turned to Star somewhat angrily: 'Do you even realize what you are saying?'

'Of course I know what I'm saying!' said Star angrily in return. 'Otherwise I wouldn't have said what I said, now would I?!' Star looked around again to see if they had any unwelcome eavesdroppers.

'I've been thinking about it a lot lately, Thomias. And I'm willing to take the risk.' But Thomias looked at the ground for a moment, somewhat bewildered. 'But... but what about your grandfather? And the learning-bench and all... You know we'll never get a proof of approval, now do you?'

'I know that, Thomias! I've already included all of that in my plan.'

'Oh...' said Thomias somewhat cynically. 'So now the female underling already has a plan... You're not referring to the route map of the forest wanderer again, now are you?' And now it was Star who stared at the ground somewhat dazedly. 'Yes,' she said in a soft, spoken voice. 'I've learned a lot from her.'

'Like what?' asked Thomias, not really sure if he wanted to hear the answer. 'Like what not?' said Star very seriously. 'You've seen the books in the hall with your own eyes, haven't you? There is information among them that we have never seen or learned about at all. There must be more out there, and perhaps...'

'And perhaps what, Star?'

'Well, perhaps my parents are still alive. Maybe they just packed their things and left one day? I have to find some answers, Thomias, and I can't find them here. I can only find them there, outside of our community...'

But Thomias didn't know what he was hearing. He knew Star's background by now, because they had talked about it many times over. And it was rumored that both of her parents had died when she was not much bigger than a toddler. And according to Grandpa Maxwell, this story was indeed true, but the man never wanted to go deeper or more substantively into that narrative. Nevertheless, it remained a vague and shadowy story. Because, how had their accident actually happened? And wasn't it very coincidental that this so-called accident had struck them both? Thomias found it all quite sad for Star; nevertheless, he tried not to interfere too much in this family issue. Grandpa Maxwell must have had his reasons. Perhaps the man wasn't much of a talker? And this grief of losing his only daughter was simply too much to bear?

Thomias could also understand that Star was trying to expose this potentially false truth. He would probably do the same if it concerned his own father or mother. Still, he couldn't help getting a little nervous. That Star was definitely not an ordinary underling. He already got that impression when he had seen her for the first time, when he had spoken to her for the first time, and now again.

Actually, every time he saw her, this haunted his mind. But what about himself? Was he to be called that ordinary? He always thought so, although he started to doubt this more and more lately. A doubt that seemed to grow all the time, and with every new conversation he had with this exciting young female-girl...

'Jeez, Star, I'm shaking all over,' was what he said.

'Well, you are not obliged to come along!' Star said, annoyed, while walking away in anger. But this was just the characteristic way in which Star was trying to get something done. She presented something to Thomias, and if he had his own doubts about the matter, she would get angry at him. And Star always claimed that she didn't force anything onto him...

But maybe that's just how she was. And maybe she didn't even realize this, given herself. But Thomias realized this little technique of hers by now, and he now had this good argument at the ready to use against her, should she once again unreasonably burden him with her plans and problems. And Thomias also knew that he would undoubtedly have to use this argument soon, perhaps somewhere in the near future, but probably more than once...

'Star, wait up!' He called Star back before she would walk around one of the many living tents, and would disappear from his sight. She came back with a pouting face, although Thomias knew her little games by now.

'Think about it,' he said calmly. 'We were almost caught when we were in the hall of forgotten knowledge. Don't you understand that this is a life-threatening undertaking? This plan of yours?'

'Well...' said Star, as she looked at him. 'I'm willing to give my life for some answers about my parents.'

'But, but...' said Thomias hesitantly again. 'You

haven't thought this through at all. For example, where do you want to spend the darkness? And what do you want to live on? And what about the forest...? The forest is immense.

We might get lost. We will...'

'Yes, I know what you want to say Thomias. We will end up just like the forest wanderer. That was what you wanted to say, wasn't it?'

'I don't know, Star,' and Thomias sighed deeply. 'The risk is just so huge. I don't carry that passion that you have in me. That all or nothing character...'

'Well...' said Star in turn. 'I thought that you too had your own passion? What was it called again? Oh yes, that you wanted to become an inventor so badly? Isn't this an excellent opportunity to aspire that? Do you have any idea what you could come up with in that vast forest further on? The many ideas and inspirations that will force themselves on you? Because... then you can really be free in your head, and you don't have to think about all that trivial community stuff.'

'I indeed want that deep in my heart,' said Thomias, 'but...'

'But you are afraid,' added Star. 'And I'll tell you why that is, Thomias. Because community life hinders you in your ideals, in your dreams, in that passion that you earlier had noticed in me, but that you no longer dare to acknowledge for yourself. Who knows what you might discover out there?' was what Star mentioned for a second time, and of course, to convince Thomias some more.

And Star also had her fears and doubts, of course,

and she would love to go out and explore together, much rather than solely on her own, but that she was going on this trip, that was for certain!

'I think there's...' and she pointed into the direction of the forest for the umpteenth time, '...much more out there than we realize. And I am simply fed up with the many questions that we are never allowed to ask. To all those rules, laws, and regulations that we always have to abide by. And to be frank...'

And she looked around with some suspicion. '...I don't trust anyone in Alfalfa anymore. And certainly not those pompous elders. They are holding something back...'

'Something like what?' asked Thomias, slightly annoyed because he was once again dragged into this, couldn't really do much about it, and at the same time couldn't resist it either.

'I don't know exactly,' said Star. 'But I want to find out about that too. Because… why are they allowed to do all kinds of things? And are we allowed to do almost nothing? Why are they allowed to dress up in the most flamboyant clothes, while we aren't even allowed to wear one small piece of jewelry?' And at the same time, she felt the wooden pendant resting on her chest again. 'But if you'd rather stay here... If you prefer to become a hut—and tent builder, be my guest!' And Star walked away in anger again.

'But?!' was what Thomias called after her. 'But what about your grandfather...? And what about my family...?'

Star worked out her plan during that darkness;

precisely as she had been doing so often lately, with the straight candle flame standing next to her nest. More and more often, she had exchanged the light outside for this illuminated darkness. Because this light, in which the people obediently carried out their industries, began to feel more and more like an act to her. And this darkness, on the other hand, was a part of the revolution in which she really felt that she was living. But to spend her entire life during the darkness was also something she preferred to avoid. And that's why she was now pinning some pillars on a piece of parchment with a little piece of charcoal. Perhaps exactly as the 'forest wanderer' always had done; slightly bend over in her personal protected cave.

She went through the key points for a moment, and at the same time felt a certain satisfaction for them. She knew exactly how she was going to handle this...

During the few revolutions that followed, she went through this plan with her bosom friend Thomias who, despite his still present doubts, also seemed to change his views more and more. Simply because Star knew what she was doing apparently, and had a clever and thought-out structured plan ready that he, as a self-proclaimed inventor, discoverer, or perhaps even engineer, could certainly appreciate. He would therefore come along with her, but only under one condition: Star would have to confront her grandfather with the book she had found in their shared vegetable garden. Because... Perhaps there was a legitimate reason for all this? And Thomias simply didn't want to undertake a journey that led to nowhere; hobbling after a phantom idea that would make them do nothing but walk in circles... Star agreed to this, although she decided to come up with a ruse at the same time.

Because, if she were to confront Grandpa Maxwell with the book; a book that was most likely written by his hand, then he would never let her undertake this journey. The man simply wasn't born last revolution, and he would know that his granddaughter wouldn't just visit another community. He would understand that she was going on a search; a search for a certain truth that this man deliberately seemed to be hiding from her… She lied to Thomias when she said that she had spoken to her grandfather about the book. She also said that Thomias' earlier suspicions were indeed correct. That her grandfather had indeed traveled through the forest as a young male-boy, and that he had indeed been to places where the unknown plant parts from the book had grown and flourished.

The man had withdrawn to the community of Alfalfa shortly after the birth of Star's mother, and he had buried the book as a reminder of times long forgotten; times when even Grandpa Maxwell had been a bit rebellious...

'You see,' said Thomias, relieved, and also somewhat elated because the perilous adventure they were about to undertake was probably a lot less 'forbidden' than he'd initially thought. The two went through the pillars of Star's plan and tried to prepare for their journey as well as possible. Soon they would leave. And the plan, and also the preparation for it, went as follows: Star told her grandfather that both she and Thomias wanted to visit Thomias' old community, the Betanex. Thomias told his parents the same thing, and together they would go to the community temple to ask one of the elders for a proof of permission, and thus a proof to travel. Thomias had agreed to this plan, and so, on one of the revolutions, they went to the temple, thinking that they had these travel documents already in their back pockets. But nothing could be further from the truth, of course… Thomias, exemplary as he was, did get a hold of one of those travel documents. For the elders could understand that he felt a certain yearning or homesickness for his old hometown, and that he would like to see some of his acquaintances and friends whom he had to leave behind at the time. But Star, on the other hand? What had that Star actually for business in Betanex?

But even when she suggested that she just wanted to accompany Thomias, and was curious about another community besides that of Alfalfa—a fairly legitimate reason, so she thought—she didn't seem to get a green light.

The only thing the elders did do, was look at her suspiciously. She didn't even receive a certificate of approval, which basically implied that she didn't even sufficiently mastered the rules of conduct that applied within Alfalfa. Star felt severely offended by this and was treated as something much lower than an ordinary novice. She was basically treated like a toddler here, who, almost always, just before darkness would kick in again, forgot to light all the candles in their abode. Hmpf, she thought scornfully, while looking at one of the haughty elders.

A while ago, she might have felt sad about this, and perhaps even shed a small tear because of this. But not anymore, no, not anymore! And supposedly disappointed, she left the community temple again, with a truly disappointed Thomias in her wake.

'What now, Star?' was what he asked, somewhat defeated, while taking a closer look at his newly obtained document. 'What's there to do now?'

But Star, bright as she was, already had a new plan at hand…

Star brought Thomias the necessities. The man-boy called himself an inventor, didn't he? A self-proclaimed engineer, wasn't he? A self-proclaimed artist, he pretended to be? Then he probably could work with this. Star had, with the knowledge she possessed, managed to fabricate a certain piece of parchment. She had managed to weave together the wafer-thin strips of stalks, and it looked like her chosen industry was finally benefiting her. She knew that the sap of this plant would act as a kind of glue, and so she had managed to fabricate a basic piece of material to write on. She had let the glued-together leaves dry, had smeared another secret ingredient over them, and had let it discolor for a few revolutions. She had then managed to cut it out to the same size as Thomias' travel document and then gave this piece of paper to him, a homemade wooden stamp with the logo of Alfalfa on it, a piece of charcoal, and a candle to use the wax from to print the logo-stamp on her self-fabricated document.

Now it was to be seen if that Thomias was really as resourceful as he pretended to be lately. But Thomias hadn't lied at all about his self-proclaimed abilities, and into the next revolution, he came up with an almost identical travel document as that of his own. Star snatched the document from his hands and then quickly rushed to her grandfather, although at the same time realizing that she couldn't show her enthusiasm too much. The man was simply not allowed to know about her actual motives...

'Grandpa! I have the travel document you wanted so badly to see!' And she handed him the piece of parchment.

'Well... That looks pretty good..' said the man with squinted eyes.

'I'm going to miss you. When exactly are you going?'

'Well, probably not the coming revolution, but the one that follows,' said Star somewhat feigned. The man put the piece of parchment away for a moment and then looked his granddaughter seriously in the eyes. Now we're going to get it... was what Star thought.

'I want to give you some piece of advice, Star, whether you like it or not.

I've seen a lot of things in my long life, and I'm glad that you now also have the chance to spread your wings some more, but I still want to give you something in your travels...'

'I'm listening,' said Star.

'Don't stray away too far from the graveled path. Visit all of the checkpoints properly. And behave humbly in the presence of the guards. The guards are there to help you move forward. Don't be afraid of them. They have us, Alfalfans, in their best interests. Besides!' And the man raised his index finger in the air to reinforce the argument. 'Keep your pendant hidden at all times. I know you're still wearing it, Star. And you also know that I accept this given, but the guards will be less friendly if you'll show it to everyone, or will flaunt with it in plain sight. Don't ever forget the rules of conduct! Including: Thou shalt not distinguish thyself from another underling by physical finery! Because, that simply implies that you consider yourself better or higher than someone else.

Remember that very well, Star. It's very important to keep in mind...'

Star nods, and she understands where her grandfather is coming from with all this, although at the same time, she doesn't understand a word of it.

She just thinks of the pendant, which she wears around her neck all the time, as a beautiful addition, nothing more or less than that. Okay, it distinguishes her somewhat from another underling, but she doesn't hurt anyone with it, now does she? It doesn't make her feel any better than anyone else. Plus, most of the time, it isn't even visible, and it's tightly tucked away; deeply concealed under her vest. Nevertheless, she decides not to go into the matter much further.

'Go and pack your things,' the old man finally says. 'In any case, I hope you'll come home soon, so you can tell me all about your experiences. And then the first meal you'll get from me will be a nice sweet tuber jar!'

Star thanked her grandfather slightly too exuberantly and gave him a small Judas kiss on his cheek. It might surprise him how long it would take for her eventual return. If the man only knew what she was up to... She grabbed the travel document, walked to the stairs of their spiral home, but decided to take a look behind her; to take a look at the man who stood somewhat hunched in the middle of their living space, while staring into nothingness and loneliness.

She felt something like a tear welling up for a

moment, but she didn't really understand why. Why now? Why at this particular moment? She really loved this man, and she hoped, and she thought, he knew that all too well, but at the same time, she also realized that some people were just very difficult to be loved. With already heavy legs, she walked up the spiraling stairs. Would they see each other ever again after her departure? Star had mixed feelings about it...

Tricky Answers...

Star prepared for the departure on the revolution that followed. She took out her large leather pouch and filled it with some basic necessities. She put the route map in it, her book full of plant life, a writing tube filled with fresh chunks of charcoal, some fruit and nuts for the road, and of course a piece of fool's gold and a piece of flint. Because, if they didn't have the opportunity to start a fire, it would be pointless from the get-go. She took a set of clean clothes with her while putting the travel document in her back pocket. She stood still for a moment, musing whether she had forgotten something, but she couldn't really think of anything. These items had to suffice. The only thing she shouldn't forget was her trusty wooden spear that lay in the bushes out there, somewhere just outside Alfalfa. It would make her feel safer and thus be able to fend off potential threats. She could hardly fall asleep during that darkness. Finally...

Now, after a whole life, finally no more community obligations and no more learning-benches. She could finally embark on a real adventure now. Finally!

Star and Thomias met in the center of Alfalfa during the next revolution. They quickly went through their inventory and then set off; supposedly walking neatly over the narrow gravel path that should lead them to their first checkpoint. They had no other option than to start from this path. Several Alfalfans now knew about their undertaking, and who knows who was watching them? The piercing eyes that supposedly stung in their backs? After walking for a while and jumping over the fence of post number sixty-six, the two arrived at the stone statue that looked exactly as they had left it last time. Star stood still for a moment… 'Perhaps we can find more clues here?' she said questioningly.

'Tips on how to continue our search?' But Thomias didn't seem to listen, and all he did was ramble in a trance… 'My name is Thomias and I have returned, together with my good friend Star, and…'

And Star quickly pulled him by his waistcoat; straight into the hall of forgotten knowledge. But when the two had stepped inside the room, with a new torch burning in Star's hand, something seemed wrong. Most of the books had disappeared all of a sudden, and that could only imply that someone else had been here, just after their own first visit to this hall. Only half-decayed parchments and tomes were left in the room. Nevertheless, Thomias found something very interesting; a book that was still partially readable, and which he immersed himself in before telling these findings to Star.

Star couldn't help but notice this, and she too immersed herself in her plant book, at the same time thinking about how to proceed from this point on. Because it was already quite clear: the two had already stranded…

Thomias briefly went through his discovered book with Star: 'This is really baffling, Star,' he said enthusiastically. 'This book is quite strange but fantastic at the same time! It seems about a world we don't know at all. A world with so-called planets and a scorching sun. A human world as we know it, only then it's called 'earth.' Funny, isn't it? Earth... That's what we call the ground which we walk on. The world that's sketched in this book is very beautiful, but at the same time very harsh. Survival seems to be very difficult, and people are completely dependent on something they call 'the weather' or 'the elements', although I haven't quite figured out what they actually mean, and...' But Star didn't seem to share this enthusiasm at all. 'And...' she said, '...Now you've already forgotten what our real reason is for coming here?'

'No! Not at all!' cried Thomias, annoyed about her remark. 'I just found it a funny story, and I thought I'd share it with you because it doesn't look like we'll find any useful clues for the time being...' And Star couldn't help but agree to this, even though she didn't want to admit it out loud.

'Oh,' she decided to say. 'It's probably just a fantasy tale, nothing more than that. Let's get to the bottom of things. There has to be something to be found here, right?' Thomias put his book away and started to help with the search. They combed through everything, read almost every letter that was legible, and picked up almost every book; even if it started to fall apart from misery. They looked into every nook and cranny of the room: they removed cobwebs, they blew dust and earth from the parchments, but there was still nothing of significance to be found. Nothing at all about the community they came from, and nothing sensitive about the elders who reigned supreme there. No landscape or route map with special locations depicted, where they perhaps could find even more special and unknown flora. Not even a story about the great war that had waged so many eras ago, or the actual circumstances for it, nothing of the sort. The trail clearly ended here, and so did the trail towards where grandpa might have been in the past, or perhaps even one of Star's parents. And disappointment struck totally when the light from outside suddenly went to black, and it just got a little extra darker in the hall...

'Damn it!' exclaimed Thomias. 'Now what?' He looked at Star questioningly for a moment, at least to the extent that was possible in this now even more darkened room. Star's torch was getting shorter and shorter, and Thomias noticed that it wouldn't be too long before it would go completely black in this little hall.

'Let's just go to sleep,' said Star, defeated.

'What? Here?' asked Thomias in surprise. 'On this stone cold surface?'

'Yes,' said Star. 'At least we are safe here. We have no idea what's going on or what could transpire out there in the dark. Just lay down on some pieces of parchment or something, those things have turned out to be completely useless anyway...' And the two prepared a place to sleep for themselves. Star had kicked out the torch during their first visit to the hall, so it may read nice for the reader. But it doesn't really make sense here. During this second visit to the hall, she hadn't kicked out the torch yet. You may decide what's most logical in this case.

Star simply had a strong sense of space, and she knew that they had waited a little too long to extinguish the torch. It had now been dark for a while out there, and that would automatically indicate that they had been very visible and noticeable from the outside of this room. Their torchlight would have been seen from a far distance, and it might have attracted unwelcome visitors; perhaps even a brave, curious man-human who, despite his superstitions, still with both eyes wanted to see what was going on with the stone beast. That terrifying monster that now also had been given a luminous mouth, and for the real superstitious out there, even seemed to spit flames for a moment...

Thomias and Star had difficulty falling asleep, and they saw this moment as an excellent opportunity to discuss their next steps for the coming revolution, and that in whispery voices. Star mainly spoke; however, as Thomias seemed to be okay with everything while he perhaps was secretly hoping for a safe return to their community. Star also couldn't deny that their plans had now changed, and her follow-up plan sounded as follows: As soon as they'd wake up, they would prepare to go to Betanex. At least, Thomias would go to that place, and she herself might just return home. Because, the fake travel document she had in her back pocket was for extreme emergencies only, not something to just go to any checkpoint with. That was a bit too risky. Even for her.

Perhaps Star should just forget about this whole adventure, tell her grandfather the lie that she had lost her travel document during her steps, and at one point, but not quite yet, finally confront the man with the plant book she had found in their vegetable garden. Just to see what he had to say to it. This would allow her to immediately clear up her biggest secret, and in that way enable her to resume her daily activities with more peace of mind, and also with a lighter heart. For there wasn't much left in this world, at least what she thought, that could sweep the ground right from under her feet. She seemed ready for any truth now, and maybe all that, via this crazy detour, was the best thing after all. And honestly, with all those soothing thoughts in the back of her mind, and lying there so peacefully in the dark, she already became at peace with that potential prospect... Thomias, on the other hand, seemed less satisfied.

He wanted Star to go with him to Betanex because he didn't want to take on that venture alone. Nevertheless, he also understood Star's point of view. Because, waving around a bit ostentatiously with a fake travel document was, of course, not really wise either. Moreover, it would be pretty noticeable if they both appeared in Alfalfa without having set foot in Betanex; without even having visited the first checkpoint... A deep sigh sounded through the darkened hall.

Perhaps it was time he'd embark on an adventure of his own. And perhaps he'd even enjoy it in the long run; walking along the graveled path while chatting with some guards occasionally. Plus, it would also be nice to speak to his old neighbor again. Because, even though the man was surly most of the time, he was also one of the most skilled flint processors in Betanex. And maybe he could bring a nice souvenir home for Star? And Thomias, too, while thinking in this darkness, more and more began to come to peace with such a prospect. Tomorrow would be a revolution in which they would do things completely different. In other words: doing exactly as they had always done before their rebellious escapades. And the two fell asleep reasonably relaxed and snoring, only to be startled the next revolution—just after the light went on again—by something heavy that seemed to trip over their perched bodies. A completely unexpected event that, even though they'd just made peace with their old fate again, would give their short-lived run a completely different turn...

'Ouch!' cried Thomias, as he jumped up quickly and in fright to see what the heavy thing was that had been lying over his legs.

A dark figure quickly scrambled to his feet and seemed to want to get away as quickly as possible, but the brave Star had swiftly picked up her wooden spear and now lightly poked it in the back of the mysterious intruder.

'Halt!' was what she said. And standing still was exactly what this creature did.

'Who are you?! And what are you doing here?!' But there was only some chuckling to be heard. 'I'd better ask you...' said the figure in a controlled manner. 'It's me! The statue! In all of its magnificence! What are you doing in my dungeon?!' But when this figure slowly turned around, while Thomias held a hand to his eyes because he had a hard time adjusting, this creature turned out to be nothing more than a male-boy... A man-boy about the same age as Thomias. However, Star had patiently been waiting to continue with this 'game'. A game that was actually played out by now, even though this boy didn't realize it yet. The male-boy raised his finger in the air in a somewhat haughty way, and stated again: 'It's me! The statue!'

'Yeah, yeah, stop the charade already,' said Star. 'I knew from the very first start that someone had entrenched itself behind that statue.'

'Oh, did you now!?' the boy said, somewhat piqued. 'Why did you take the stone monster so seriously then? Why did you respond to the questions that the stone statue asked you...?'

'That you asked us...' said Thomias dryly, but the unknown male-boy looked back at Thomias somewhat poisonously.

'Oh, look who's suddenly all brave?' But Star tried to temper things.

'It's all right, nothing is the matter here,' she said. 'We aren't your enemy, and it looks like you aren't one of us either. Now, do tell us. Who are you exactly? And what are you doing in this place...?' But the boy sniffed his nose for a moment and then searched around the hall as if he was looking for something.

'Was it you perhaps?' asked Star. 'Were you the one who removed most of the books from this place, not so long ago?'

'It was I indeed,' said the boy, without looking up or back, and without even mentioning his name once.

'Do you and that clumsy person standing next to you have a problem with that?!'

'Clumsy?!' said Thomias. 'Take it easy, man...'

'Easy? Easy?! I don't have the time to deal with your kind at all! Why did you have to stay here for so long in the first place?! You two are the first in a very long time who have dared to stay here for a prolonged period. I only came here to pick up my book. Where is that godforsaken thing anyway...? The only reason that I'm here right now, is that I've lost that darn thing somewhere; otherwise, I would have never returned!'

'Is this perhaps what you're looking for?' said Thomias triumphantly, and he pulled out the book from behind his back, which he too was beginning to see as his personal possession.

'That's mine!' shouted the unknown boy, while Star once again tried to temper things with some hand gestures. Now they all could be detected, but these two ruffians just didn't seem to care… 'And now it's mine!' shouted Thomias in return. 'Unless… unless you tell us how marvelously clever we are…'

'Huh?' And both Star and the mysterious man-boy looked at Thomias in some amazement for a moment. 'I'm referring to the questions we answered a little while ago. We had them all correct, now hadn't we?'

And Thomias stood as proud as a peacock while the unknown boy mocked him in his face.

'Whaha!' he laughed. 'You don't even know half of it, boy, and that's taken literally!' Star stood with her arms folded, looking at the two young boys.

'Well, then explain them to us,' she said. 'I mean, you desperately want your book back, don't you? And when you're done with explaining those questions, you can also explain in detail why you wanted to snatch all these precious knowledge-valuables from under our noses.'

'Good…' said the boy in his characteristic way, and this didn't seem to escape Thomias. This boy was indeed the stone statue…

'Okay, where shall we begin… Look, I'm a

philosopher at heart, although that probably won't mean that much to you. Nevertheless, you may still call me by that name. I shall allow that. That's fine by me. I'm also endowed with a photographic memory. Not only can I fully trace back our previous conversation. I can even see every spoken word dance before my immaculate mind's eye. You will start!' And the boy, who apparently called himself the philosopher, pointed theatrically and somewhat haughtily at Thomias. Then he pressed his index finger against his own forehead. 'Pho-to-graph-ic Me-mor-y...

According to you, the strange thing about water is that it can take on any form or shape, even though it doesn't have a natural form of itself, right?' And Thomias nodded proudly. 'Wrong! The anomaly of water is that it has a higher density in liquid form than it has in solid form, and you two could've never gotten this question right, because you two poor bastards have never been familiar with the phenomenon that's called 'ice formation.' Star indicated with her posture that she wanted to say something, but the philosopher only looked at her somewhat contemptuously. 'Question number two! And that brings me to you, young female-girl. A very simplistic answer, although that's not entirely to be helped, because underlings are quite simple and also quite rudimentary creatures by nature. A very simplistic answer indeed...' the philosopher said again. 'Although, and ironically, you weren't that far from the absolute answer at the same time. So, and I'd really have to admit, not that bad, not that bad at all...'

And he gave Star a smooth wink while saying it. Something she seemed to be more receptive to than she'd initially thought. There was just something about this newly acquainted male-boy that seemed to appeal to her. The boy was tall, at least a lot taller than she was, although that was only something physical. It was more because of his attitude, of his presentation so to say. And whether this could be depicted as arrogance or just too much self-confidence, she couldn't exactly point out either. But she found it quite something. Yeah, it definitely had something. And the fact that he seemed to know so much, only seemed to contribute to this interesting picture. And moreover, he too was clearly different than most... The philosopher continued: 'What, or who, has always been, always will be, and will always remain? You! Star, wasn't it? You answered that it was nature, because nature will always be, will always remain, and will always blah blah blah. Now, you weren't too far off of the right answer, also. Nevertheless, you couldn't have known this answer either, because 'the cosmos' or 'the creator' is simply no longer a concept within those retarded and simpleminded communities from which you may or may not come from. Nevertheless, nature is of course also a part of the cosmos, of the great and driving creative force, and it indeed comes, goes, and remains. Besides!' And the philosopher blew some dust from a torn piece of parchment that he held in front of him like a true thinker, and that he also gazed at for a moment. 'In the past, and that for a very long time ago, people believed in nature as the divine creative force... So, if you look at it in that light, you got the question actually somewhat right...'

'Ha!' said Star, and she clapped her hands cheerfully.

'Well, no need to be so cheerful,' the philosopher

said bluntly. 'Almost everyone could've come up with that answer. I mean... have you ever taken a good look at your surroundings? Nothing but nature and plants! Last question... And of course, this one I can also remember vividly and crystal clear.

What human aspect is both his greatest blessing as well as his greatest curse? Now, I just know that you have argued about this among yourselves; it can hardly be otherwise. Nevertheless, it was you again Star, who came up with an adequate answer. According to you, they were the thoughts of a human being, right? And even if you got the question somewhat wrong, you actually got it somewhat right also. Clever, babe. There seems to be something powerful slumbering within you; an intuition that you could be proud of. It's a shame that you have to lower yourself to a life within one of the communities. In that way, you'll never be able to reach your full potential, of course. But that aside!

I'll explain to you in detail how things work around here, so I can get MY book back, and can continue on with MY path. The greatest curse and also the greatest blessing of a human being is, of course, his own consciousness. But the man-boy didn't give the two any space to contemplate about this...

'Here with that book!' was what he immediately said.

'Hold up!' said Star. 'Not so fast! You haven't explained at all what you're doing here precisely, or the reason why you've removed all those books and parchments...'

'What I'm doing here seems quite clear,' said the philosopher. 'To immerse myself in the forgotten knowledge that lies within this place.' And the boy pointed around for a moment. 'I mean what used to lay here.' And he had to chuckle at his own remark.

'But why did you remove them in the first place?' asked Thomias this time.

And the philosopher leaned forward for a moment, while holding his hand beside his mouth, as if this information was only intended for them.

'I'm on to something,' he said in a soft, spoken voice. 'I come from a community not too far from here. And what I've discovered is that this hall of knowledge is situated in an exact straight line; that it's located right behind our own community temple. That must mean that many eras ago, this must have been some kind of library; located adjacent to that same temple.' And the philosopher paced through the hall again for a while; searching for something in a way as if he couldn't find what he was looking for. Then he turned to Star and Thomias in a somewhat theatrical way. 'It must be here somewhere,' he said. 'A sort of entrance; a tunnel that should lead all the way back to my community...'

'That may all be true,' said Thomias dryly again. 'But you still haven't told us what you've actually done with all those books. Because Star and I were very curious to read them, and that probably goes for many other underling who dares to take a step in this forgotten hall. Star decided to take over:

'And what is that name exactly? Of that community you supposedly come from?' But the philosopher pretended to look for a certain tunnel again. Nevertheless, this unknown and somewhat mysterious man-boy, also knew that he'd better come up with something good if he wanted to get his precious book back. He looked to the left for a moment and then to the right, while he spoke to the two in a smooth manner: 'I'm here on a secret mission,' he claimed. 'I come from a place called Deltarion, and I was given the assignment to collect the forbidden knowledge from this hall. A new elder has joined our community recently, and he's planning to do things entirely differently. Moreover...' And the boy rattled on in an incoherent way, while Thomias decided to hand him his book, just to get rid of all his yapping. The story of the philosopher seemed to become more and more unbelievable with every word that came out of his mouth. Yet, he told it with such persuasiveness that Star and Thomias couldn't tell whether he was telling the truth or whether he was completely fooling them. Nevertheless, the three had been so absorbed in each other for a while now that they'd no longer had an eye for their surroundings. They were so absorbed in one another that they didn't seem to notice that they had been surrounded for a short period of time; surrounded by a group of somewhat rough-looking men. Thomias was suddenly harshly grabbed by the lapels of his vest, and Star was also firmly grabbed by the wrist. The two screamed out in fright, but it was already too late; they had been discovered… One of the men, the presumed leader of the bunch, looked at the philosopher with anger on his face. 'What are you still doing here, boy?! I've told you earlier that I didn't want to see your face around here anymore!' The philosopher seemed to want to escape as quickly as possible.

And now, like a weasel, he tried to look for a real tunnel across the room, although he too seemed to have no chance of fleeing. The only exit was the mouth of the stone monster now, but even he, as grand as he presumably thought he was, was indeed too big for that small gaping cavity. 'Who removed all of the books?' asked another man suddenly. But the leader, whom these men called 'the commander,' decided not to respond. The message was therefore short and clear: the philosopher had to make a run for it, and the commander never wanted to see him in this place again. And would that happen again in the future, then the outcome would be a lot less rosy for him next time. The philosopher quickly made his way, with the weasel tail between his legs, and without looking back at the two underlings he actually didn't know at all, whom he'd only just met, but with whom he already had shared such exciting conversations.

'Bah!' said one of the men. 'It reeks of scum in here!' Another man had to laugh for a moment. 'Yes, and you know what we always say, don't you?' And the group sang in unison: 'We simply don't want rats in our midst!'

The two bosom friends didn't really know what verdict hung over their heads. Nevertheless, their search seemed to be over by now; that was for certain. They were harshly put against the wall of the hall, and their wrists were firmly tied behind their backs with some sturdy rope. And for them too, the message was simple and concise: They had to come along…

The Choice of a Sunflower or a Painfully Stinging Cactus

As they walked along, and wherever they were taken to, they were constantly addressed by the man who was still being called the commander.

'Who are you?! Where are you from?! Which branch or division do you belong to?! And what is the code word?!' were some of the things he asked. But poor Thomias seemed unable to speak from shock, and even the normally loose-lipped Star could hardly get her words out. She had no idea what these men wanted from them, and what the commander exactly wanted to hear. What she did seem to notice was that these men didn't wear the traditional costumes of an average checkpoint guard. When it became clear to the commander that there was no sensible explanation or answers to be gained from these two trespassers, a cotton bag was suddenly, and quickly, pulled over their heads. Thomias screamed out for a moment, although the only thing that came out from under the bag was some low, muffled sounds. The boy was now seriously confused. Where was he? What was he doing here? Were they caught? And had the light outside already gone to darkness again? The poor guy let it all be after a while, and there was only silence to be heard from under the bag.

After walking for a short period, they came to a

halt… Suddenly, there were voices and some laughter to be heard in the distance, and Star, with her keen hearing, could also hear a campfire crackling; telling her that they had ended up in some type of community. The cotton bags were removed from their heads, and the two hostages were pushed into a small, makeshift prisoner room.

A wooden fence was put in front of the basic confinement, and it was tied firmly with some sturdy rope to block their way. Thomias suddenly collapsed and began to wail in desperation. Star was still standing proudly; however, stood upright, and confronted the commander, who stood stately in front of her, with the improvised closed wooden gate in between them.

Star wasn't afraid, she knew that they were basically screwed, and she didn't know exactly what punishment was hanging over their heads, but she did know that if the elders would punish them, she would at least have an effective rebuttal ready. She looked quickly behind her. Luckily! Her pouch with her personal belongings, and more importantly, containing her evidence, was thrown into the cell with her.

'Do you belong to that boy that calls himself the philosopher?' the commander asked calmly, but Star denied. 'No,' she said. 'We don't know that man-boy at all. We've only spoken briefly to each other. He…' And she didn't really know if she should say this at all, but decided to say it anyway, because perhaps they would be treated with a little more leniency. '…He pretended to be the stone statue…' A mysterious grin adorned the commander's face for a moment.

'And you thought that was quite interesting, didn't

you?' Another man had joined the two in the meantime, but Star shrugged her shoulders questioningly.

'We were just curious about the knowledge that was in the hall,' she said honestly. 'We didn't really understand that much of the things that male-boy said in there.' The commander seemed to think about this for a moment, although he was disturbed by the man who had come to stand next to him.

'Ha!' this particular man suddenly added. 'Knowledge! Always that damn knowledge! Knowledge is mainly the reason why we live in this way now!'

'Shut your mouth!' said the commander quickly. 'But commander... it surely is the truth, isn't it?' But the leader of the two had his rank for a reason, of course, and he also understood, and that better than anyone, that in a situation like this, one should never show the back of his tongue so immediately, and certainly not when dealing with potential spies... The two men suddenly and promptly walked away, leaving Star and poor Thomias with nothing but questions...

'We are from Alfalfa!' shouted Star after them.

'Please take us back there!' but this cry of despair seemed to be in vain...

Star turned around and pitifully looked down on Thomias for a moment.

'Well, I guess we'll just make it easy for ourselves in the meantime, now won't we?' And she knew that it might be a bit harsh to say at this stage of their run, but indirectly she wanted to indicate that she regretted taking Thomias along with her on this trip. The man-boy clearly wasn't suitable for an adventure like this.

Because, even if one was caught, the best thing to do in the end, was to speak to your captors as neatly and as clearly as possible. Nevertheless, Star also sat down on the ground despondently, and with her head bent between her knees. Perhaps Thomias' reaction was quite normal? And perhaps she was the odd one here? Because, the fact that this didn't even affect her that much, could only mean that she carried a certain fatalism within her.

She had become somewhat indifferent during the passing of so many cycles, although at the same time seemed to embrace this aspect of herself. It seemed to keep her going; it kept her standing in situations like this one...

She looked at Thomias with pity again; situations in which an average underling seemed to crumble apart in misery. She grabbed her pouch by touch. Fortunately, she always had her evidence with her. Now did she...? Or...? She quickly made the hole in her pouch a bit bigger and then looked in the bag in horror. The book! Her book of unfamiliar plant life was gone! She threw the pouch angrily through the cramped wooden cell, in which she almost hit Thomias' head with it. No evidence to show anymore, no strong arguments they could put forward to back up their story, none of that.

Now it was indeed nothing more than waiting for their reckoning. She hated this miserable world! She took a quick look in Thomias' bag, but that one was also empty... Just before they had left home, they had quickly gone through the things they would bring along on their mutual trip, but she hadn't really seen any palpable stuff from him at all. Would even Thomias have lied to her? Would he perhaps have taken nothing with him on their journey at all? Except for his, permission to travel, ticket? Thinking that their adventure would be nothing more than an innocent walk in the park? Literally…? Or would someone now rejoice over their illegally obtained valuables? Oh well, Star didn't care that much about it anymore. They, whoever they may be, were allowed to have these things by now. That they may be happy with these possessions and gloat about them. But Star did know one thing for sure: she and Thomias would probably never see their items back again… Thomias had regained composure after a while, and was now even reasonably approachable. But just when the two wanted to enter into a dialogue with each other, about their sudden imprisonment, about their lost belongings, and what exactly to say to the elders when arriving back to Alfalfa, the wooden fence was suddenly loosened with a lot of fanfare, and they were prompted to come along. The two were then guided through a small encampment… There was still a large campfire crackling, and the looks of the men sitting by the fire followed the feet of Star's group closely as they walked by. The group walked past several tents and all, so it seemed, were provisionally set up and made of a variety of animal skins. It gave Star a somewhat poor impression, on the other hand. Either, these tents were indeed made in a hurry, or these men-humans weren't very skilled in their assigned industries. However, she soon withdrew this view when they held ground at a somewhat larger, and also much more qualitative, tent. What kind of place was this?

It didn't seem to be a community, and it certainly wasn't Alfalfa either. Was this perhaps a temporary stand for appointed guards? Those who skimmed through the forest in search of straying underlings? The group walked into the big tent... Soon their pressing questions would probably be answered...

They were both allowed to sit on a wooden box. Opposite to them sat a man at a separate wooden seat; the same kind that the forest wanderer had been sitting on, while handling her writing quill, and Star shook her head incomprehensibly. She didn't even know this piece of furniture, or even knew of its name, and yet people still had them in their possession. What exactly was going on in this forest? The man sitting opposite looked at them with piercing eyes, while holding his hand on a certain book. 'Hey! Those are our...' Thomias tried to say, but he received an admonishing tap on the back of his head from the commander. 'Silence! Nobody!' he said somewhat harshly. 'Let our leader speak.' And the man opposite to them cleared his throat.

'So...' he said. 'From what I understand from my assistant, you have nothing to do with the boy who seems to call himself the philosopher?'

'We don't know that man-boy at all,' said Star again.

'Splendid!' said the man, and most likely the leader of this entire encampment. 'Yet, there seems to be something not quite right here.' And the man tapped his fingers a few times on the book in front of him. 'Indeed, we have to be careful with rats in our midst,' another man said, with Thomias suddenly jumping up from the wooden box he sat on. 'Ha! That's exactly what he said earlier!' And he pointed to the man who had just given him a slap across the head. Thomias seemed to carry some bravado in him all of a sudden, and it was probably due to his long-running inner tension that now came out as a form of rebellion. The commander looked at his superior for a moment, slightly mumpish and embarrassed. 'It's alright, it's alright,' the supposed leader waved at him reassuringly; a man who was also dressed in high-quality clothing, and decked out with shining ornaments. 'This is what it's all about,' he said, while tapping on the book again. But Star knew it was all too late anyway, and she'd better clean up her act right now. This man clearly sympathized with the elders, he even looked like one, and she told him the entire truth so that he and his associates could hand them over to Alfalfa again. She told him their story in broad strokes, with the final conclusion that they both were looking for a certain truth; a truth that they just couldn't seem to find within their own community... 'Please don't punish us too severely,' was what she added. 'I can tell from you that you are an elder. Please bring us back to Alfalfa again. We will keep a low profile for the coming ten cycles, I promise you. We didn't want to get in the way of you elders with our strolling through the forest. We meant no harm with this little subterfuge. We have family waiting for us. I have a grandfather to take care of... And...' And Star clearly started to get emotional.

'Well... You should have thought about that earlier,' said the supposed elder somewhat unreasonably. However, the man also looked at Star with a certain twinkle in his eyes. 'But why do you think I'm an elder?' he asked. And Star took a quick look at the man, from his head all the way down to his toes.

'Well... It's just...' she said hesitantly. 'About the way

you're sitting there in that unknown seat. Because of your clothing style. And because of the decorations dangling on your robe that no one else in the communities is allowed to wear.' The man complimented her on her strong perceptual ability, and he also said that she indeed wasn't far off. Nevertheless, that was a matter for later. For now, he wanted to talk about the unknown author of Star's confiscated book. 'So...' said the man, after hearing Star's short version of her story. 'So, you think your grandfather is the writer of this book?' And Star nodded.

The man leaned over for a moment and then looked at the cover with pinched eyes, 'The letters *MB*...' he said, somewhat surprised. Quite strange that the writer has put his initials at the bottom of the book. Very unusual indeed... And extra special that this person apparently put himself out there with two names... May I know your grandfather's name?' And Star told him his name. The man seemed to be startled for a moment, although, and at the same time, also managed to maintain his self-control. 'Just what I thought... I already had such a suspicion...' said the man. 'At least, if it's the Maxwell I've once known...

I can't make a statement about him though, because it could be someone else, but the Maxwell I once knew, and that for a long, very long time ago, was indeed, and just like me, an elder... And if so, I also think I know about the origin of this second name...' And Thomias', and especially Star's ears, began to ring at this still concealed secret.

'But...' said the leader after his statement. 'I absolutely can't tell you this name. For this unknown author will have to remain unknown for a while, until we know for a fact who it is exactly we're dealing with here. Because, it's quite easy to point the finger arbitrarily, but there are already enough false allegations and misconceptions circulating within this world; and one of the main reasons for the emergence of the Great War so many eras ago. And we don't want to go through that again, now do we?'

The leader of the encampment looked at the commander for a moment and he also nodded in agreement. 'I assume this is your property?' he said while giving the book back to Star. 'Apparently, this is your burden to carry. And these items are probably yours. Aren't they? Quiet boy?' And Thomias was also happy to take back his personal belongings. 'You two are a bunch of oddballs,' continued the man, while smiling at Thomias. 'You have manufactured some funny weaponry, boy.' And Thomias seemed to glow for a moment at this unsuspected compliment, although Star didn't really understand what this was about. The man shifted in his seat and placed his hands comfortably on the back of his head.

'A bunch of oddballs indeed, but actually not that very different from us people here.' And the man decided to tell them the background of this entire encampment. An explanation that he granted the two because of their alleged character; because of their honesty and their candor. The man had indeed been an elder once, although he had now distanced himself from that office. Simply, because he agreed less and less with their method of working.

He and a few followers had joined another group of 'forest wanderers,' and thus had managed to form a coalition; an ever-growing splinter group that in turn consisted of smaller groups, and who all adhered to their own particular freedom and convictions. They even had certain ranks among themselves, like the commander for example, and they were tolerated by the ruling powers of the other communities, as long as they didn't interfere too much in their activities and affairs. This ex-elder, and also one of the highest leaders within their movement, apologized to the two for all of the fuss, for all the commotion, and also for the earlier distrust in their personas. His faithful men seemed to see ghosts behind every tree these days. 'Can you imagine how many ghosts that must be? With all that many trees in the forest?' was what he joked wryly. But there seemed to be something else that this man was holding back from the two; something that hadn't escaped Star's notice, and she decided to ask about it...

The man looked worriedly for a moment, then looked at his assistant for advice, but the commander himself looked somewhat resigned, and then shrugged his shoulders. The leader thought again for a moment.

'I'm not sure if I should tell you this,' was what the man said. 'But it seems that the seed has already been planted within the likes of you, and on top of that has even started to sprout somewhat.' And this man, who had been sitting across them for quite some time now, would not only not hand them over to Alfalfa, but would even give these two underlings a clue that could turn their little world upside down; an unexpected clue out of an unexpected corner. It was the continuation of a guideline that they had initially searched so diligently for, but unfortunately hadn't been able to find yet. Now, and suddenly, they were given a veiled clue that could make them choose between two distinct worlds, and that literally...

'The seed has already been planted within you two,' said the man again.

'But it's up to you whether you leave it partially in the ground, and scatter bits of earth over it, as time passes, while slowly forgetting about it. Or that you decide to give it some water and attention, while letting it bloom into a meter-high sunflower. But beware!' was what the man also added.

'Instead of a sunflower, a bone-dry and painfully stinging cactus could also emerge from that soil. In other words: this choice, and also this risk, is entirely yours to make and take...' Star looked at the man inquisitively for a moment. This man seemed to speak in riddles, and that gave her a sign that he indeed must have been an elder at some point. However, also an aspect that she'd never been able to detect in her own grandfather. He, on the other hand, was very straightforward and very clear in his statements. The only thing that was somewhat comparable was that Grandpa Maxwell also seemed to be hiding something; seemed to carry a certain burden with him... But hey! Star carried such a thing around too. Was her grandfather perhaps not the unknown author of her book after all? Star began to feel slightly confused again. Still... she just had to know... What was it exactly that the leader of this splinter movement was talking about?

'I have...' the man said, contemplating, '...Even though you may not have thought so at first, a great respect for your flight. In my view, it testifies of a 'staying true to yourself,' and to a certain desire for freedom; ideals that we also try to pursue in this encampment. Still, I'm going to tell you something now and you can't talk to anyone about it, would you decide to return to Alfalfa...'

Thomias held his homemade weaponry in his hand and then nodded in agreement. However, Star looked at her trusted comrade questioningly but also somewhat proudly. Had he suddenly and tacitly accepted this quest? Was there a certain bravery dormant within him after all? Even that Thomias was still a bit of an enigma to her. But if even he agreed to this, then of course she had no choice but to join him in this choice. They would face this together; two soulmates who seemed condemned to one another, with no longer having a problem with it whatsoever. And Star, in a stylish way, also nodded along without adding anything else to the matter. The man told them about a mysterious barricade, a long walk from here. A high barrier that seemed to keep something out, or perhaps something in. A gate, so it seemed. A gate that even the men of this splinter movement had never passed. The sturdily built commander added that, even though they seemed to live in a certain false freedom, that was still better than having no form of freedom at all; or to live within a totally controlled environment as took place within the communities. They simply didn't know what was out there, and they really didn't want to know either. 'Because...' so the man wisely stated again, '...sometimes it was better for an individual not to know everything...' But Star and Thomias seemed to be people who wanted to know everything, on the other hand. And even though Star felt slightly confused for a moment just now, and everything seemed to turn out to be nothing at all, the pieces of the puzzle now suddenly, and especially after the explanation of the leader of this splinter movement, started to take form a bit, or at least, became a little more visible. And even though they were still missing a lot of puzzle pieces, and the pieces they did have were still completely mixed up, Star also knew that this puzzle had to form a certain image somehow and somewhere; somewhere far away from here... An ideally defined picture where both she and Thomias could immerse themselves in with a certain serenity. Within an ideal world in which there were more answers than questions. And in the most ideal scenario? A place where there wouldn't be any questions at all. Only answers and mutually expressed suspicions...

Heat and Cold

After walking for a long time, while following the route that the leader had pointed out to them, they indeed ended up where they needed to be.

They had managed to bypass a number of checkpoints; the small guarding posts they had seen very little in their lives, but those were less manned than they'd initially thought, and for the most part, they could walk right past them; half hidden in the bushes and with the low fence along the graveled path as their indicator. Now, however, they had reached a point where they were forced to stay tucked away in the bushes, simply because there was something in front of them where it was impossible for them to show their faces.

Thomias whispered to Star: 'Look at that, Star. We've already seen a lot by now, haven't we? But something like that?' And Star also gazed in awe at the immense gate which, and if correctly seen from this distance, appeared to be half open.

A gate that seemed to be made of some type of material that they'd never seen before, while it shone a bit like fool's gold, in Star's opinion.

A meter-long and also very high gate, entirely made of a type of material, at least as it seemed, for which she always had to knock on the door of the elders in the community temple with supplications, while crawling on her knees, figuratively speaking. *What an exorbitant opulence!* Thought Star. *And what a slap in the face of an ignorant underling...*

Large, wide tubes of the same material sprouted right next to the gate and thus partly disappeared into the forest ground underneath. Where did these weird pipes go? And better yet, what was their function? And also Thomias wanted to know all about it. But just as he wanted to inform Star about it, a loud and also deafening tone suddenly sounded. A red light flickered from all sides all of a sudden, and the many parrots, geckos, howler monkeys, and various other animals seemed to flee quickly into the bushes and treetops because of this. Star quickly pulled Thomias down, now even deeper into the vegetation.

'What is this?!' she whispered in a fairly loud tone. 'Have we been discovered?!' But the sound got louder and louder, and at one point it was so plangent that the two couldn't help but put their hands over their ears. They saw how the guards walked towards the gate with quick steps, and how most of them then disappeared through the gate again. Only one more deafening alarm tone sounded. And then? And then the light outside suddenly went out...

Now it was almost pitch black where the two had been hiding, and nothing more than a strip of light seemed to infiltrate this thicket; a little light coming from a light source that kept shining near the gate.

'What is all this?!' Thomias asked Star helplessly as he put his hand on Star's back in a somewhat childish way, but also as a reference point.

'I don't know!' shouted Star in a moderate tone.

'Let's wait and see...'

The two remained quiet for a while, and so did the environment. Occasionally, there was a scream of a howler monkey to be heard in the distance, or a high-pitched cry of a macaw, but for the rest, only the insects, and especially the crickets, seemed to fill the space with their sawing wings. The larger animals had fled deeper into the forest. They had withdrawn a bit more towards the communities; there where the people already were safely lying in their nests. And Star also thought for a moment whether it wouldn't be wise to do the same. The behaviors of animals were simply a good indicator, and perhaps it was safer to follow their example? On the other hand, this large shining gate also seemed to beckon them... Because, why did it stand there in the first place? And... What could actually be behind it? It was quiet for a long, very long, time now, and nothing seemed to happen at all in the vicinity of the gate. The darkness had once again taken over from the light, and except for the crickets, all life, including the guards, seemed to have completely withdrawn. At one point, Thomias had had enough, and he got up from his hiding spot: 'I've had enough of it, Star!' so he said. And he walked out of the bushes in a nonchalant manner; towards the half-opened gate. He turned around for a moment. 'I don't feel like hiding anymore, Star. Let's just see what happens... And if I do get caught, I will have my word ready. I'm just going to say that I'm on my way to Betanex, that I've lost my way, and that I thought that Betanex was perhaps behind this gate. In any case, I have a valid document to back up my story!' *And he waved the piece of parchment triumphantly in the air. But?!* Thought Star. *He doesn't even have any valid stamps! No stamps that would indicate that he at least had visited one checkpoint! The guards would never fall for it...* But the stubborn Thomias had already made a run for it. *Numbskull!* Was what Star thought, but it was already too late, of course... Thomias became smaller and smaller, and she saw how he had arrived at the gate, looking for a guard to speak to; looking for his own downfall that he didn't seem to realize himself. Star held both her breath and her heart. The light in the distance flickered up again, so that the now reduced Thomias sometimes disappeared for a while and then became visible again. After a while, however, she thought he was waving at her. Did he want her to join him, perhaps? She quickly looked around, not a soul in sight...

She took a big, deep breath and then ran as fast as she could, and as silently as possible, towards her brave but oh so reckless companion. Because, if they were to be caught, then it would have to be both of them...

'What do you think you're doing?!' she whispered with a semi-loud voice to Thomias, who, however, held a finger against her lips and then pointed towards the darkness behind the half-opened gate. 'Let's go,' he whispered. 'Apparently, and for whatever reason, this is our chance.' Star looked at him worriedly for a moment. 'I'm not sure...' she said. But Thomias waved with his travel document again. 'You have one too, Star, remember? We are on our way to Betanex, aren't we?' 'But what about the checkpoints?' Star said. 'And the...?' But Thomias already pulled her along by her vest, right into that pitch-black darkness...

After running for a while, Star put her arms around her body and made clear to Thomias that she wasn't feeling very well.

'Why is it so cold here, Thomias? This doesn't feel very pleasant.'

But Thomias didn't want to hear about it, and suddenly it was as if the roles had been reversed. An argument that he put forward because of the much earlier pulling of him into her madness; the pull into her personal quest. 'Come along now, Star,' was what he said. 'Now we're going for it too.' But even poor Thomias, driven by a certain impulsiveness and perhaps also by a certain fatalism, couldn't exactly have known what he'd gotten himself into. Nevertheless, they kept walking; walking towards a certain nothingness, simply because they couldn't see a hand in front of their eyes anymore. Star let herself be carried away by this slight compulsion. She had indeed asked for it herself, she was indeed the instigator of all this, and backing down now would firstly be nothing for her, and secondly, a form of hypocrisy. And even though one could say a lot about her, she absolutely didn't want to lend herself for the latter.

The roles had now been reversed, and now it was she who kept a hand on Thomias' back so as not to lose sight of him. And even though the two walked blindly on and on and, without actually realizing it, were burning their own bodily energy in order to keep their bodies warm, Star continued to find it deathly cold... At one point, they stopped walking. Star felt far too cold by now, and even though walking might've been better, they had stayed awake for an entire revolution by now, and resting was perhaps the wisest thing to do at this point. Moreover, something strange was going on. The light seemed to be getting closer and closer in the distance, and also seemed to warm her in a special way. Nevertheless, Star felt more and more miserable. And whether this was because of the cold, or that they'd really gone a bridge too far with their escapade, was difficult to say, but for the very first time she began to seriously doubt this subterfuge that, certainly in her opinion, could now cost them their lives...

Thomias, on the other hand, started to see things in a somewhat brighter way. But now that this strange light started to gain in strength, he too couldn't help but conclude that they'd found themselves in a very desolate and also very barren landscape. A landscape where it would be very difficult for them, if at all, to find any food. Yet, there was also something else that took over from him; a kind of revelation that made him see things in a much broader perspective. Thomias seemed to feed his bodily energy with these newly acquired insights, and he wanted Star to go along with it; no matter how cold she might feel at the moment. Nevertheless, he also knew that Star was now in a state of panic, in a certain shock perhaps even; just as he had experienced so himself when they had just been caught by the splinter movement. And he also realized that Star could now think of nothing else but their shortage of food. About this strange new world that now surrounded them. Whether they ever would be able to find their way back home. And whether they would stay alive at all. Thomias had suddenly acquired a certain knowledge on the other hand: crucial information taken from the book of the mysterious philosopher, and that he hadn't told Star about yet, because he hadn't had the chance to do so, but also wanted to wait a bit longer. Star was clearly hypothermic at the moment, and if Thomias had an extra thick cardigan, he would certainly have wrapped it around her body, but unfortunately, he hadn't brought one along, and the only thing he could warm her with at this moment was with some uplifting positivism, and with his newly acquired knowledge. Star, however, was just murmuring in front of her: 'Grandpa, I'm sorry... What is this whole world really about?' And.. 'It's so cold here... So cold... What kind of place is this? Are we going to die here...?' Thomias tried to keep her awake as best as possible, and to distract her somewhat, he spoke to her encouragingly: 'Look at this here now, Star. Can you see that lightbulb in the distance?' And he pointed towards a piece of a luminous sphere that seemed to be getting bigger and bigger by the moment. Above them flickered all kinds of beautiful little lights that kept Thomias both captivated and wide awake. 'I've read about this, Star, I swear to you,' was what he said. 'I am therefore of the opinion...' and he pointed again towards that fraction of lightbulb in the sky, that now had somewhat increased in volume, '...that I've read about this in the book of that weird boy. That there, in the distance, must be a planet, Star. And if that is indeed the case, then this, the ground we are sitting on right now, must be that which is called 'the earth.' In other words: a world completely different from the one we are coming from...' And Thomias rattled enthusiastically on about the knowledge he had acquired from the philosopher's book: About planets, about clouds, about stars, and also about the climate. And even though Star seemed to have dozed off a bit by now, she had heard all of his sayings with her razor-sharp hearing. She slowly opened her eyes and then looked into the blinding ball that was hanging just a little above the horizon. 'What a strange light it is, isn't it?' she said softly. 'Who could've made it? And how did they manage to place it up so high? It even gives me some warmth, and it's so bright that I can't even look straight into it...' Star seemed to be completely absorbed in this illuminating sphere, and it gave Thomias the impression that she hadn't fully understood the message he was trying to bring her. However, Star understood very well what Thomias was trying to tell her, although she simply didn't agree with him. She insisted that the book he'd read was nothing more than a fantasy tale. That this world in which they now wandered was a make-believe world; created by fellow underlings, and that the world they'd just come from was the real one. Thomias reassuringly put a hand on Star's forehead, while checking her temperature at the same time. But even though her forehead felt stone cold, he could also feel some clammy sweat on his palm of the hand. Star had a fever by now, and she seemed to be somewhat delirious because of it...

He thought for a moment whether it was a wise thing to do, but then decided to take off his own vest. In any case, he still felt fine, and if he did get sick because of this, it would probably take a while before the malaise would reveal itself to him. He stroked Star affectionately over her head, and then put his vest over her body. He took some of his belongings out of his bag, and then began to tell her, as silently as possible, about his inventions: something he had never done so before... 'Star...' he said. 'I've always told you that I wanted to be an inventor, but I've never shown you anything concrete, actually...' He took out his little weaponry, while Star already seemed to be in a deep sleep. 'I call this a slingshot,' he said. 'It's a V-shape of branches with thickened vegetable resin from the rubber tree stretched in between. It works quite well. I can shoot projectiles like pebbles with it, and perhaps I could catch some wildlife with it in the coming revolution, or whatever that's called in this world. We really won't have to starve to death, Star. That I promise you.' And he put the weaponry back in his pouch. He looked at Star as if she was still wide awake, although she now had a satisfied smile on her face, and had sunken into a deep slumber.

'I noticed how you'd looked at me, Star, the very first time we'd met.

And even though you may not believe that I carry an inventor in me, I, just like you do, also look at the world in an exceptional way. For example...

I learned that if you rub a piece of animal skin very quickly through both of your hands, the piece of skin starts to get warm. And if you then hold this piece of animal skin close to your arm, miraculously all the hairs on your arm will rise and stand up. This must mean, Star...' was what he thoughtfully said, '...that in that moment a certain attraction takes place. I have thought about it a lot, and I therefore believe that our body seems to radiate something, but what that should be, I don't know exactly... But I've thought of more things Star, because just like you, I also have my unanswered questions. For example, water seems to diminish more and more if one leaves it standing in a bowl for several revolutions. How can it diminish all of a sudden? And where does it go? Moreover, it also seems to become less and less when it's put over a fire, only then the strings come off, protruding in the air; crinkles looking like thin wire... Where does that phenomenon come from? And why does that also disappear into thin air? What is it exactly? And how does it all work...?' Thomias dropped his pouch next to him with a thud. 'Perhaps we'll never know the answers to these questions, Star, but I am willing to follow you to the end of this world for it, nonetheless. And even if only one of our questions were to be answered, even then I would be satisfied, as long as we at least got one of them right. That's all what matters to me...' The brightly shining sphere had now climbed even higher, and Thomias saw this as an excellent opportunity to take his own rest; there in that ever-increasing heat. And even though Star didn't agree with him prior, delirious or not, make-believe world or the real one, at least some things were now fairly clear to Thomias. The philosopher had spoken of a creative force, a cosmos, and Thomias almost dared to claim that he had a fraction of it in his head already, although he would tell Star about it another time. For now, however, the most important thing was to fall asleep. Because, even though it felt somewhat unnatural to do so in this ever-increasing light, there was of course nothing more unnatural than not embracing sleep at all...

In the course of that day, they woke up drenched in sweat, and instead of Star feeling so cold, she now had to throw off Thomias' vest to avoid complete overheating. Star had been thirsty for a long time, but now she suddenly felt hungry too. She had been very cold for a long time, but now she suddenly felt very hot; with her clothing sticking so annoyingly to her body. There was no worse way to step out of a nest than this, and that was exactly what she did.

She was very grumpy, very touchy, and the sight of this desolate landscape only added to that. And it was poor Thomias who had to pay the price, of course, although the boy seemed to miss this completely. And when Star suddenly and proudly stood up out of a certain frustration, Thomias only saw this as a sign that she was doing much better currently. Thomias still felt great, and as a rattlesnake's tail, he started rattling at her; something he'd said to her before actually, but which he tried to make very clear again: 'Star... It's unbelievable...,' was what he said, 'but something strange seems to come over me. Because, the more I start thinking about these things, this world, you know, the clearer it seems to become to me. I would almost like to say that I have a bit of the cosmos in my head already...' and Thomias had to laugh jokingly at himself for a moment, and then decided to respond to this saying himself. He looked at Star from an angle, and still with a smile on his face. 'But don't let the philosopher hear about that...!' And even Star, despite her bad mood, had to smile at this for a moment. 'No, indeed...' she said. 'How would he actually fare? Where would he hang out at the moment? He really knew a lot, didn't he? Actually too much for an ordinary underling...' But Thomias had no intention of talking in depth about that conceited blowhard. Because, even though he had started talking about him himself, he also detected a certain jealousy within when he saw how Star's eyes started to sparkle when they talked about this mysterious boy. Nevertheless, her mood remained like a thunderstorm. And these invisible clouds over her head only seemed to increase as a sweltering day passed, while it alternated again in an icy-cold night. The two seemed to be walking around aimlessly;

walking on these dusty grounds where not even one blade of grass seemed to grow. And when Thomias, with great pain and effort, and with his bare hands, had tried to dig a deep hole, he hadn't even encountered a single earthworm... A very bad omen indeed, and also an indication that the groundwater had to be much deeper within, if these grounds contained any water at all... Not a single bird flew through the air, and no larger animals were visible, or smaller animals audible. It was only rocks and boulders that they had encountered in their steps, and of course, that big sweltering ball that seemed to follow the two in its annoying way, and that kept them forcedly company. They had even turned around out of a form of desperation; towards the great gate that had brought them to these infernal grounds, although they couldn't find it anymore. They had already strayed too far. That was very clear by now...

What in the name of the cosmos had ever possessed them to walk this far? So deep into a pitch-black, and also stone-cold world, that they knew nothing about at all? Their adventurism had clearly gone over their heads, and they now had to pay a far too high price for it; a presumable death due to dehydration...

They now sat almost completely dehydrated and also exhausted against a pile of boulders that had once again randomly appeared in this strange landscape.

Random rock formations that gave them the ominous feeling of walking around in circles; some type of strange Twilight Zone in which the same things constantly passed by. Poor Star really felt like she was about to go off her perch, although she would only give in to that after she had told Thomias her somewhat unreasonable truth. She snorted with her nose and then started to speak:

'Ugh!' she said with disdain. 'Inventor? Inventor!? Inventor of nothing at all, is what you are! I haven't seen anything of you yet, except for that ridiculous V-shaped toy of yours. How do you, in the name of that cosmos of yours, ever want to catch something with that? Dust perhaps!? Or some of these annoying rocks that lay scattered around everywhere? You should've invented something that could've helped us on our way! A method with which we could have found a source of drinking water!' Star felt provoked, and tears now rolled over her cheeks. She knew very well that they would die here, it was now only a matter of time, and death would probably visit them earlier than expected during this strange darkness. She also knew that her words were harsh and unreasonable, and that she too was partly to blame for the demise of the sweetest boy she had ever known. But this was just how powerlessness came out of her; in Star's own characteristic way. Thomias' eyes also became watery by now; the little bit of fluid that his body could use so well at this moment. He just couldn't understand these villainous and unreasonable words from Star, although, and at the same time, he also realized that he had failed. He had not been able to protect her, and he had indeed turned out to be an inventor of nothing, and was actually not even worthy of this title. Yet, he thought he understood this world much better by now; this world in which they had been walking for a number of 'revolutions', and which he claimed he had already encapsulated in his head.

And even though he was almost certain that that strange light source in the sky had to be 'a planet', that the ground they were walking on was called the actual 'earth', and that this cold had to be part of 'the weather', he could now ironically and wryly do nothing with it, or use it to their advantage. Star's words were very unreasonable, and not entirely appropriate, but perhaps that was just the way in which female-humans expressed themselves every now and then? In any case, he didn't feel any resentment for it. She was she, and he was he, and they just had to make do with that, no matter how long they might have at this point...

The fiery orb in the sky had now almost completely sunk and disappeared behind that strange line in the distance. Star had dozed off again, and despite her earlier short rant, she now had a peaceful and calm expression on her face.

Nevertheless, Thomias, and with the few powers he still had within him, realized all too well that she might remain stuck in this sleep if he didn't do something soon. The boy did something he had done before and used the following motto for it: 'it's only really over when everything goes to black,' and according to him, that wasn't the case yet. He put his vest, which he could've used for himself because of the advancing cold, over the sleeping Star again, and then gave her a kiss on her cheek. 'I'm sorry, Star...' he said. 'But... But I have to find a source of water... For us two...' And in his far too thin undercoat, he started walking, with now suddenly another mysterious planet in the sky that seemed to miraculously, and in a silvery manner, illuminate the path under his feet. But Thomias, brave as he was for doing this, didn't last very long, and after walking for a whole good hour, he also collapsed through his knees. His mind still wanted to go, but his body just refused. The poor boy simply had no more energy left to power his body becoming increasingly heavy. And he now only thrived on the necessary nutrients that kept his constitution alive and his vital organs functioning, while laying there so helplessly, and with his mouth half open, on this dusty and also bone-dry surface. The only thing that seemed to haunt this plain was he himself; along with the tormenting thoughts in his head that managed to taunt him even more, while he was reminded of a paraphrase he had taken from the philosopher's book, which he had managed to remember, and of which he was now painfully reminded:

The world called Earth...

A world that is considered as very beautiful by many, but also to be considered as very harsh...

Beautiful? thought Thomias in frustration. *Beautiful?!* He had never seen anything so desolate and pitiful in his life! But one thing that the book had mentioned was definitely true: the earth was very harsh and was considered very heavy by many... And Thomias now also felt how he was slowly losing consciousness. *Considered as beautiful...? Nothing could've been any farther from the truth... I'm sorry, Star... I have not been able to protect you... I have failed...*

The Hidden Valley

Thomias woke up after a few days, at least, he thought he was awake.

Nevertheless, he wasn't in some spirit world that the philosopher had spoken of at the time, while pretending to be the stone statue. But Thomias also didn't seem to be in that desolate landscape anymore, since he no longer felt warm but also no longer felt cold. Actually, he felt quite comfortable right now. Was he back in Alfalfa perhaps? In Betanex, maybe? He could be anywhere right now, really. In the company of the splinter movement even? He tried to think for a moment. At least, as far as that went. In addition... he hadn't been alone all this time, now had he...? 'Star!' Thomias quickly got on his feet, while a few unknown men rushed towards him. 'Star?!' He shouted again. 'Star?! Where is she?! Is she still alive?! What did you do to her?!' But one of the men laid a hand on his shoulder in a reassuring way. 'Don't worry, young boy,' was what the man said. 'We have found the one you speak of. However, she's still in a deep sleep at the moment. You are in Meriva now. Here you will be safe...'

A blanket of reassurance fell over Thomias, and he placed the back of his head with a thud on the soft, raised surface that he had been lying on for all this time. Here they were safe, apparently. He would soon know where he was exactly, but for now, he decided to close his eyes some more...

During the few weeks that followed, more and more became clear to the two. Star had almost recovered by now, although she didn't seem entirely the same as before. Thomias was wide awake, on the other hand, and he tried to support her as much as possible; wherever he could.

It all had been too much for Star, so it seemed; the many impressions and changes that had followed each other in a rapid succession:

The pretense of the communities, grandpa's alleged lying about his true identity, and their brief imprisonment within the encampment of the splinter group. But also their wandering within a pitch-black world that she had depicted as an illusion, while considering that of Alfalfa's as the real one. Her inner fight to stay alive, the very long sleep that she could hardly remember, and now this again... Again, waking up in a whole new world to which they would have to adapt. A world which resembled the green, lush environment where they originally came from, although this one too had an entirely different name and location.

Star now wandered in front of Thomias like some sort of zombie, and that aspect didn't escape the inhabitants of this green area either. They would soon get her mind back in order. Although, they also thought it would be wisest to do so gradually... There was still a certain reserve among these inhabitants, however.

And soon they would give this girl all the answers, but not before they exactly knew with what sort of meat it was they were dealing with here. And that applied to both her and this young boy, who now walked through their green, glorious, lush, and also sheltered living environment with eyes as big as ceramic saucers… And so it came about that these two figures were playfully taken by the hand, and were shown a piece of this new world in a friendly manner; a world that lay somewhere half hidden, in a beautiful and also very green valley. The inhabitants called this piece of land Meriva; a place intended for the very few freethinkers who still remained in this world. People who decided to dwell in this hidden valley, and who adhered to the doctrine of the cosmos with all their might. Or, as they called it: the doctrine of the great creative force, while trying to maintain it as best as they could. While, at the same time, fighting against another great power, which seemed to be advancing all the time, and that was getting bigger, more influential, and more powerful by the day…

And while these two Alfalfans were taken gently by the hand, they slowly were taught this basic knowledge; about the, at this stage, still accessible knowledge to these Merivians, but also information about the artificial world they themselves came from. It was on a day like this that their regular tour guide took them in tow, and gradually showed them the way within this real world…

'My superior has given me a number of instructions,' said the friendly guide.

'He is of the opinion that we can tell you a bit more about it by now. Nevertheless, I advise little Star to stay to herself, might the information become too much for her at some point. Walk along with me, and I shall make some things clear to you. At the end of this run, there will be a surprise waiting for you, something that Star will certainly appreciate, and that might even cheer her up a little… But to get straight to the point: The two of you, and many alongside with you, have spent their entire lives, or certainly most part of it, in an immense greenhouse; an immense dome with its own artificial climate, and also flora and fauna…' But the man already held his footsteps in for a moment.

'No…' he said. 'That's not entirely correct. The animal and plant life within this dome were indeed very real, only some sort of machine was built around it to be able to feed these life forms. Hm…' the man said again. 'Machinery… You two aren't very familiar with that concept either, now are you?' But Thomias claimed he could follow the picture reasonably well so far. He also thought that he understood this concept 'machine' by now, and he immediately referred to the large gate they had seen and passed at the beginning of their search, and those strange shiny pipes protruding from its sides.

'Right! Very good!' said the man. 'That is indeed some type of machinery; a small part of that large installation that we call 'the dome.'

The three walked on again; over unpaved walkways through the landscape, and along agricultural fields where multiple groups of playing children hobbled after a bunch of young animals. The guide walked in front of the group, and he told exuberantly and candidly in his steps. Thomias mainly nodded, sometimes asked for a further explanation, while aiming his auricle at every word that came from this guide. Poor Star was noticeably struggling at the very back of this small gathering, however; mainly concentrating on the greenery around her, and perhaps even wondering if she indeed had died, and now had ended up in some sort of paradise.

Thomias still informed her about some things, but for now, he tried to concentrate as best he could on the words of this Merivian guide that seemed to confirm his earlier suspicion; a suspicion he'd already had when they, in a lonely way, had walked through the barren and also desolate landscape. A suspicion that had known its starting point when he had found and picked up the book that belonged to the mysterious philosopher.

However, the guide now mainly talked about the ins and outs of the dome. That it was an immense geodesic—self-supporting—structure, and that the climate within was fully regulated in order to achieve a stable sub-tropical climate; a climate that made the specific plant species in the dome grow and flourish. Water was supplied by a complex and ingenious pipe system that took care of irrigation, and the light and the darkness that followed had to serve as a certain artificial order; serve as an order and thus also as a daily schedule, through which the underlings would imagine themselves in their physically real but also, and not realizing it themselves, make-believe world… Thomias' throat became bone dry when he heard all this, and he was glad that Star walked a bit behind, because he was of the strong opinion that this wouldn't do her mental state any good at this point. The guide looked at Thomias for a second, and Thomias looked back for a moment, although what he saw in the man wasn't a happy facial expression at all. However, the guide still tried to remain a certain smile on his face.

'Didn't you find it strange that there was so little diversity of plant and animal life in your particular dome?' But his small grimace disappeared as quickly as it had come. 'Oh no, another faux pas on my behalf, you guys have never known any better, now have you? Gosh... You two really have to reinvent the wheel completely, now don't you? Wheel...' And the man shook his head again. '...You guys don't know that concept either... This is going to be a long one...'

But Thomias told the man somewhat rebukingly that, even if they did come from such a dome full of ignorant underlings, it didn't automatically imply that they were a complete set of morons. And their guide had to laugh at this remark. 'No! You are absolutely right! My sincere apologies! But if you've stayed here as long as I have, you forget about such aspects more and more. You should know boy, that I've lived in such a dome too once. And like you two, I've also managed to escape, and was eventually taken in by these freethinkers. And now I use the knowledge that I've accumulated about the dome-community that I used to live in, to their advantage. You could almost say that I am the best of both worlds!' And the man had to laugh again at his own joke. 'And that's also the reason why our spiritual leader has appointed me as a Merivian tour guide, and because of my smooth way of talking, of course...' And Thomias expected another burst of laughter from the man, but strangely, it didn't follow.

'So, you also had to completely reinvent the wheel? Prior to coming here?' was what Thomias sharply asked.

'Well, that wasn't all too difficult for me,' said the man. 'I was able to get a lot of information from the knowledge-corner of our community temple...'

But Thomias scratched his head when he heard

these phrases.

'Something's not right,' he stated. 'If the domes are supposedly so concealing, why wasn't that the case in your community?'

'Another good question!' the guide pointed out. 'I've never really thought about it in that respect. I just thought of myself as an exemplary underling, while performing my industry as neatly and as diligently as possible every revolution.

Nevertheless, I was just able to immerse myself, and that without any form of resistance, in certain knowledge-matters at the time. We were absolutely not allowed to leave the area, and we had to strictly adhere to all the rules of conduct, but for the rest we were given reasonable freedom in that area...'

'But why have you decided to leave then? If you were such an exemplary underling?' But this question came from an unexpected source all of a sudden, and Thomias turned around in surprise when he heard that this voice came from nobody else than Star! Star had only heard the last part of their conversation probably and that, according to Thomias, might have been for the best. The guide looked at Star doubtfully for a moment. 'Well...' he said. More and more people started to disappear at a given point, or became seriously ill.

It was said that they were taken to other places, but to where exactly wasn't discussed. As submissive underlings, we weren't allowed to talk about such delicate matters. I just didn't want to get as sick as so many others, so I just packed my belongings and left. I would be lying if I hadn't expected more opposition, but strangely enough, they just let me go. They were also special times back then, perhaps things just went differently in those parts? You know what?!' the man suddenly added. 'I believe this is enough information for today!' And he looked at Thomias again for a brief moment. 'Try to explain as clearly and as calmly to Star what we've discussed this afternoon, okay? Our surprise can wait until tomorrow.' The man gave the two a friendly handshake and then walked off.

That evening, Thomias caught up with Star near a small campfire.

A bonfire, only intended for them as an exception to the rule, and to give them some space to catch up and organize their frame of reference.

'There are a number of things that don't add up, Star...' was what Thomias somewhat clumsily said. 'I think I know what you're referring to, Thomias, but perhaps it's exactly as the tour guide said? Perhaps things were just slightly different in the past? At least in his time?'

'Yes... Maybe...' said Thomias. 'But still... something doesn't seem right...'

'No shit, smarty pants...' said Star somewhat sarcastically. 'Nothing seems right anymore with all this, now does it?' And Thomias snorted his nose. 'Hmm, you're certainly right about that. But it's just so strange that, especially at that stage of these so-called domes, he could find out about such knowledge-matters so openly...'

'Well, I don't know about that either, Thomias, but there could be several reasons behind it. Perhaps the rules of conduct weren't so firmly tightened in his time yet? Or perhaps it was a cunning tactic to see who carried a rebellious disposition? Or maybe it was a little more relaxed and loosened back then, than it is now in our time? It could be anything Thomias...'

'You certainly have valid points there, Star. Very sharp of you. You almost seem to be back to your former self. My compliments...' And Star slightly had to blush because of this. 'But still...' said Thomias. 'There seems to be much more going on with those domes, it just has to be.' 'Well... perhaps we'll find out, Thomias.'

'I hope so,' said the man-boy from Betanex finally. 'I really hope so...'

'Well, goodnight then.' And Star gave him a playful wink.

'Yes, sleep well, Star.'

'Oh, wait! Before I forget!' said the guide. 'I have been instructed that I'm not allowed to say anything substantive for the time being, because, and according to my superior, I have already said a bit too much. You will therefore have to show your loyalty in one way or another. In what way our leader meant this, or how he wants to achieve this exactly, I will leave in the middle, because it's not my place to interfere in such matters. The thing I can do, is show you this here: our surprise! So, pay very good attention, Star, because I'm already of the impression that especially someone like you will appreciate this kind of stuff...'

And the man took them to a beautiful, almost idyllic place; a lush, natural green strip, located in the middle of this 'hidden valley,' which he called the 'physical garden' without any hesitation. It soon became clear why this green strip of nature had been given that name. 'Come along,' said the man. 'I not only have knowledge of the domes, but I also have quite some knowledge about the many crops that the ever-advancing nature has to offer us. So, let me introduce you to our physical vegetable garden.'

'Physical?' asked Star with interest.

'Yes, most definitely,' the man said in return. 'Physical, is what I call it a bit jokingly. And even though I have received certain instructions from my superiors up above, I'm still allowed to tell you all about it. Pay very close attention, Star.' And the man pointed around him. 'All these crops seem to have a special effect on the human body and I call this phenomenon...' And the man straightened the collar of his vest, ' ...the mimicry of vegetables.' Take this vegetable, for example...' And the man pointed towards an orange vegetable that they called a carrot. 'If you cut this root in half, and you look at its interior, at its cross-section, it looks exactly like the human eye. And the scientists at Bastion have indeed discovered that these roots greatly improve the blood flow of the eyes and their sight function... And this one here, for example!'

And the man enthusiastically pointed out another vegetable. 'Although this could also be named a fruit, but that's beside the point I'm trying to make here. The tomato! A tomato has four chambers and is of course red, and our heart also has four chambers and is reddishly colored. The white coats in Bastion have therefore been able to show that tomatoes are full of a dye they call Lycopene, and that they are therefore a power food, for the heart as well as the blood...'

And so this man, who could certainly call himself a competent guide, spent the whole afternoon pointing out vegetables, legumes, and all sorts of fruit...

Grapes hung on a bunch in the shape of some human organ. The walnut resembled a small brain and strangely had a bit of the structure of this thinking organ. And kidney beans also had a healing effect on, how could it be otherwise, the kidneys, and, according to this guide, maintained the functionality of these small and tender organs. Celery, pak choy, rhubarb, and many other vegetables resembled the likeness of bone structure, for example, and also promoted the workings of the uterus and cervix.

Figs were fruits that promoted the mobility of the male sperm and prevented sterility, and olives were beneficial for the ovaries of their female counterparts. According to the guide, citrus fruits resembled the mammary glands of a woman, and according to him also had a positive influence on their tissue fluid.

The man took them through this miraculous piece of greenery all afternoon, and it indeed lived up to its name. And whether Star was completely convinced of it all, was another matter, but she had always assigned the plants and their components magical properties, and she thought it was nothing more than wonderful to hear about all this. And true or false? She tried to believe these biological givens as firmly as possible, in any case.

The guide stopped for a moment when they had almost reached the end of their tour. 'Finally!' shouted the man, almost too enthusiastically. 'The onion! And we all know of its existence, now don't we? Perhaps you've called it the weeping tuber? There in your communities? Or the children's head with the cheeky quiff? I really don't know... But I do know that you people attribute funny words to common stuff down there. Anyway... The onion... Onions seem to remove the waste products from bodily cells. They are the tear catchers that clean the epithelial layers of the eyes at the same time, and on top of that,' and the man briefly raised a finger in the air, 'also helps their workmate 'leek' to remove wasteful products and dangerous radicals from the body...' The man turned around his axis, spread his arms widely, while spontaneously smiling at both Thomias and Star.

'Well, come on, people,' was what he said. 'All this 'mimicry' can't just be a coincidence, now can it be...?'

The two had been living in this area for at least three months now, and they had learned much more about the dome they'd come from, and also about the other apparent domes that had to be situated somewhere in the vast world.

They had now become acquainted with the ideas and visions of these Merivians in a scholastic way, and it couldn't be any clearer that this hidden valley - which bore the name Meriva - was in close contact with what they called the great and divine creative force; the cosmos that Thomias so haughtily pretended to have encapsulated in his head already. The natural city of Meriva, and its inhabitants, the Merivians, had transcended superficial earthly thinking in their own way, and they seemed to do everything in synergy with their environment.

The environment resembled that of Alfalfa, but on a much higher scale.

The inhabitants were many times freer, and their civilization also seemed to function on a higher level; on a higher scale, so it seemed. Star was therefore rightly amazed, and if it wasn't for the physical garden, it was for the separate 'industries' in which the Merivians completely distinguished themselves. In which they distinguished themselves from a community like that of Alfalfa, that of the Betanex where Thomias came from, or that of the other three communities situated within their dome: The Gammanon, the Deltarion, and of course the capital Epsilonia. All three which they had never seen up close, let alone visited. Meriva, also known as the 'hidden valley', was indeed a beautiful place and Star would have preferred to stay there and become a permanent resident. But what became so characteristic for their search, was that changes followed each other in a rapid succession, and when they had just become reasonably accustomed to their new circumstances, there seemed to be another twist of fate looming in between. The two friends just weren't allowed to take it easy, and this all began to feel like a maelstrom in which they were slowly being swallowed up. Nevertheless, the next big change would only make itself known to them after the guide had shown them the tour completely, and after they had seen this natural society in almost all of its splendor...

The Merivians engaged in actions and 'industries' that a simple person could only dream of—if they had the courage to cherish such dreams at all—and the inhabitants of this valley knew how to express themselves in the most exuberant ways. They made various ceramic figurines, for example, but also large and colorful cave murals; artistic expressions that depicted their daily lives. They made sculptures of voluptuous women with large, broad thighs that were to depict the fertility of life. For their paintings and murals, they used the finest brushes made of animal hair, or they painted by only using their fingers to depict the animals they sometimes hunted. They also, and especially to Star's great surprise, had a great deal of knowledge of the natural dyes that could be found everywhere in these parts, including iron oxide, lime, and charcoal: The colors red, white, and black that they seemed to use the most. But the Merivians also had, and that to the great amazement of Thomias, managed to 'catch the light', and they could always summon it with their skill and carry it around with them. The Merivians called these light sources 'lamps'; a translucent shell of some sort of matter, unbeknownst to Thomias and Star, in which animal fat was ignited. And even though this may smelled terrible, this light source was portable and could be lit and extinguished at any time and any place. Thomias thought it was a magnificent piece of inventive art, and he thought it was a pity that he hadn't come up with it himself. But as with everything, something only seemed obvious when it was stuffed in front of someone's face, and in this case, Thomias was no exception to that rule. Glassblowing was indeed a whole art in itself, and the spiritual leader of Meriva would tell them the finer points about it eventually, but not before he would tell them a bit more about the world they'd just came from. In addition... not until they had shown their loyalty to him somehow, and not until they had shown the inhabitants of this lush hidden valley their true colors...

The leader of this hidden valley, who of course was

a freethinker himself, and was even called a grandmaster by the Merivian people, gave the two a somewhat rigid impression, although he didn't beat around the bush at the same time.

The man seemed to be wearing a heavy yoke around his neck; a certain burden that both Star and Thomias knew nothing about, but soon would also weigh down on their shoulders.

The grandmaster was somewhat in control in this valley. He had already fired the friendly guide at the two, and he was of the impression that they were now ready for another eye-opening confession. This grandmaster told them more deeply about the so-called Apocalypse; also known as the great war. The spiritual leader told them the shocking truth that this great war hadn't raged many eras, or even hundreds of years ago, but that it actually only had been going on for half a century, and that it was still raging on behind the scenes today. And the man decided to tell them about the dome they came from: the dome with its five distinctive cities and within each city, also called a community among underlings, a strict and dominant hierarchy of four designated ancient sages who were called the elders were appointed. According to this grandmaster, these so-called sages knew exactly what they were doing, and what was going on, and they therefore had a tacit knowledge of the outside world; the world outside of these artificial manufactured domes.

So-called pseudo-sages that formed a certain congregation, and that maintained close ties with an even greater technological power; a power that seemed to hold this entire world in its grip. A large group of 'wise men' who once had been freethinkers and grandmasters themselves, but who had now exchanged their integrity for a certain form of power. 'A group,' as the grandmaster described them, '...who believed they were wise and highly intelligent but were nothing more than a bunch of fools eventually. A group that...' as the grandmaster continued, '...still applied a number of rules of the freethinkers within their belief systems, even though only done by a fraction of them.'

And according to this leader of Meriva, friction and corruption also found their way within this 'circle': some still with some reasonably good intentions, and others with much, much more sinister agendas. And...' the man finally said, '...there are even speculations being whispered that these domes are nothing more than a...' But the man held a finger to his mouth for a brief second, as if what he actually wanted to say wasn't allowed to roll over his lips. As if he had to remain silent for whatever particular reason...

'Enough!' he suddenly exclaimed. 'I've told you two far enough by now. We have saved you from dehydration, we have patched you up and shown you our hospitality, and now the time has come for you two to live up to that trust.

Kindly show us your loyalty, kindly show us your added value to our society, because Meriva is simply too precious to reveal its many hidden treasures to just any wandering soul out there...'

The grandmaster kept looking at them expectedly, and Thomias in particular didn't know how to tackle this ordeal. Should he show this apparent transcended individual his infantile little weaponry? Look at this V-shaped thing, mate? Loosely fabricated from the resin of the rubber tree back in Alfalfa? It's almost falling apart by now, and I haven't been able to hit even a single mark with it yet? Something like that? This man would chase them out of Meriva instantly; back into that dusty and also inhospitable void moon landscape, with that red-hot planet above its grounds that always seemed to haunt them so annoyingly within their steps. No, they had to come up with something very good, and Thomias secretly hoped that Star would do that this time, because he himself didn't really have a clue how to do so at this point. Star, in her turn, thought carefully and with patience: *Hmm, showing loyalty...*

She told the man for the umpteenth time her story; flavored with both her and Thomias' inner quest, although this didn't seem sufficient enough for him either. She tried to compliment the man on this beautiful valley and that both she and Thomias were now beginning to understand the true essence of the divine creative force behind it, but that also didn't provide a satiating answer to this grandmaster. Star now also understood less and less what this man wanted to hear, and out of nervousness, she started to pick at her wooden pendant a little; at the small wooden hanger that she wore under her sturdy vest for as long as she could remember. 'The pendant!' she suddenly shouted, with the spiritual leader looking up questioningly; not entirely expecting there was any surplus value to be gained from these two wanderers, except for two extra hungry mouths to feed. Star quickly removed the pendant from under her collar and then showed the man her necklace; a necklace that actually consisted of nothing more than a string of rope with a small wooden figure dangling from it.

'Where did you get that?!' the man shouted loudly, causing him to lose the wise and also sober impression he had managed to maintain all this time. And Star told him the story behind the hanger. It was a piece of imagery that had meant so much for her during her short-lived life already; functioning like a small beacon of light in a somewhat dark and uncertain existence. She told the man that she had received it from her grandfather; transmitted through his own daughter; Star's late mother. It was one of the few belongings she could call her own, along with the book by the unknown author found in the vegetable garden adjacent to their mutual treehouse, and she shoved the book forward to give her story some strength. The man pushed the book aside, without even having glanced at it, and then pointed admonishingly at the wooden pendant dangling down between Star's fingers.

'I see...' said the man mysteriously. 'I think I'm beginning to understand now...' 'You've maneuvered yourself in quite a difficult position, young lady, and only time will tell which blood it exactly is that flows through your veins...

A very peculiar twist of fate, indeed... And I'm still not sure where or how I should place you, and that's why I have decided, and that with immediate effect, that the two of you should go and take a look at the huge technological city not too far from here: the city that we Merivians call Bastion. Go there, and you might find more of your answers. Because, if we Merivians know one thing for certain, it is the following: Blood always runs thicker than water...'

But Star couldn't fully grasp the words of this leader. Blood runs thicker than water? The technological city called Bastion? And why did this grandmaster behave so distant all of a sudden? She couldn't really appreciate his tone of voice. But Star wasn't in a position right now to appreciate or not to appreciate anything at the moment, bluntly put. These people had done an amazing job by patching her up, and even though she would have liked to stay here, perhaps even live here in this valley, it seemed like she wasn't entirely welcome here either, with her supposed 'background.' And she even started to believe that there was no place for her at all that she simply could call home; a place that she could fully embrace, and that would do the same in return. Bastion was apparently their next stop in their ever ongoing pursuit of the truth, whatever that truth may be. A technological city? Was what the leader had said? Technology? Hadn't Thomias used that term a few times prior? And even back in Alfalfa? Perhaps it was a place where Thomias could come into his own? And perhaps there was a possibility of becoming permanent residents there? Star could always join Thomias, could always accommodate him, because, let's face the facts, he wasn't that bad to have hanging around after all…

As short and concise as the grandmaster was at the beginning of their conversation, so minimal he was now in his choice of words: 'Good,' said the man. 'The preparations will soon be made. Tomorrow morning, I will give you a Bastian Seal; A license needed to move freely within this vast technological stronghold. Or as we prefer to call it: the vast pool of sorrow. Behave as inconspicuously as possible, and avoid as many confrontations with the police patrolling around. And if you guys, for whatever unlucky reason, are being retained or imprisoned, then say that you've stolen these Bastian Seals from one of their citizens. Because! And in addition, and so automatically a warning for the likes of you. If the unlucky event were to transpire that you two are indeed spies, and have abused both our hospitality and our trust, we will hunt you down, and kill you on the spot, if we ever catch another glimpse of you again…

Our society is currently in a truce with Bastion, and we'd like to keep it that way for as long as possible. Leave tomorrow morning, preferably even sooner, and do not return to here. As soon as the first strips of light enter our valley, two guides will be ready to escort you two towards Bastion. For now, out of my sight, because, even though this may be a serene community, and we adhere to the great creative power here, we have much more to do than taking care of some stray cats while pampering them…'

Bastion

Star's courage sank completely in her shoes, at least, in the shabby moccasins she wore on her feet. The immense and also imposing stronghold that the Merivians called Bastion stretched in both length and width as far as the eyes could see. Many lights, probably all artificial, shot into the air from all sides and angles and seemed to almost kiss the sky. The two friends still wore their old clothes, the raggedy old textiles with which they had left Alfalfa at the time, although, according to the grandmaster, that couldn't do much harm. Because, even in this gigantic technological society, there were still a handful of oddballs fluttering about: people who still adhered to a certain primal feeling. Such Bastians were tolerated, often openly mocked and ridiculed, but nevertheless permitted, and most of the time left alone. It seemed to confirm Bastion in its conception that this primal feeling was indeed nothing more than an inferior thing. Yet, 'a feeling' that, just like their own technology did, always tried to maintain itself in some way or form. This city was overpopulated with, if to believe the Merivians' estimation, almost two million inhabitants. And even though Star felt a bit uncomfortable at times, due to the many eyes that seemed to be focused on them, Thomias found this whole experience more astounding by the minute. A feeling that only seemed to grow as he began to understand the idea behind Bastion even better and more clearly; about the many inventions that were openly displayed here, and of which many already had been put into use. They now carried a Bastian Seal with them, and also had some currency in their pockets, to be able to spend at least fourteen full days here. And that's exactly what they did; spending their days while taking a good look around.

The contrast with the world they'd come from was almost bizarre, and also to be called over-excessive; the difference between this technological world, between their natural world, and that of the smaller and also somewhat larger worlds that they had seen, experienced, and traversed up till now. Thomias had the cosmos somewhat stuck in his head already, and now his sense for 'technology' was also aroused, and he therefore behaved like a small boy playing the leading role in some adventure novel; a certain writing that he once so fervently had hoped to be able to open. No, and even better, a book that he would have preferred to have written himself, with his inquisitive mind as a pen and with his cerebral fluid as ink.

Star now, and for the second time during their adventure, hobbled despondently behind her big old friend who enthusiastically pointed out everything that raced past, lit up, or towered high in the sky, before their noses.

Things that, strangely enough, and in his apparent ignorance, Thomias also managed to explain reasonably well. The two had never really known real time, only eras, cycles, and revolutions, but the inhabitants of this city, on the other hand, seemed to have grabbed this real time by the horns. They wore things like telephone watches; small devices of which they couldn't only read the exact time and date, but with which they even could talk to one another, simply by bringing their wrist to their mouth. The Bastians considered this a mere toy, almost an antique gadget, but for the two Alfalfans, it was almost something magical, and especially Thomias wanted to know how this little gadget actually worked and operated. Nevertheless, the Bastians didn't really have much time on their hands, even though, and ironically, they wore it on their wrists, and most of them quickly walked on, and didn't look back, when they saw these two eccentrics asking for an explanation. Because, such Bastians were of the impression that, even though these two oddballs didn't fully conform to the crowd in terms of clothing style, they could at least move on with the times!

But there were many more technological gadgets that overwhelmed the two Alfalfans, and if it wasn't for these talking watches, then it was for the holograms that stood on almost every street corner, and to which many Bastians were talking animatedly. The two decided to look for such a strange talking hologram themselves; one that also happened to function as a city signpost. Star looked inquisitively around for a moment. Are there perhaps more people coming from the outside? Taking a look in Bastion? And where would these people actually come from? But these were questions that she didn't have an explicit answer to at the moment. The hologram explained to them, in a somewhat childish way, how this immensely large Bastion worked and operated, and Star thought she finally understood the function of this holographic image, and in particular its tone. Because, this hologram wasn't intended for outsiders at all, or even for tourists, this childish tone was of course meant for, yes, for children: for the little Bastians who still had to find their way in this big bad grown-up world. And Star quickly looked around again to see if it wasn't too conspicuous that two teenagers now stood still next to this piece of machinery, although not a single Bastian seemed to look up or turn around anymore, and Star had now almost forgotten about her earlier paranoia and suspicions of these citizens regarding their clothing style. Because the inhabitants of this city may have grasped actual time, at the same time, time also had a grip on them so it seemed, and she tried to keep this fact well hidden in the back of her mind without entering into a further dialogue with Thomias about it. In any case, it was the first point of criticism that Star already had about this strange, almost bizarre, but also ambitious living environment...

The hologram continued talking and almost everything was discussed, including the earlier seen telephone watches and even the various holograms that could be encountered around this technological city. Holograms that they'd now already become familiar with.

In turn, portable devices were powered by mini batteries that never seemed to run out of energy, and larger public objects, such as these hologram machines, simultaneously scanned their surroundings in order to extract useful information from citizens that passed by. Or, as the hologram itself called it: 'In order to automatically contribute to a cleaner and more user-friendly living environment...' And even though the two Alfalfans had been standing next to this talking machine for quite some time now, and had listened to many of its short stories, this apparently was only theme one…

Star had heard enough by now, and she wanted to explore this metropolis on her own again, although the now almost enchanted Thomias seemed to stop her in her impatience. In his opinion, this was a treasure trove of information, and by spending one more hour here, they would be able to learn much more about Bastion than by wandering around aimlessly for the upcoming days, while their limited currency would slowly but gradually dwindle. And even though Star knew he had a legitimate point, she also had a point: a pointed head, so to speak. She had enough of these holograms by now, and she hadn't experienced anything as boring as this in quite some time. Thomias held a firm grip around her wrist however, while playfully forcing her to listen to theme two of the hologram's presentation…

Theme two was about the construction and also infrastructure of Bastion's architecture, and Star couldn't help but think of the industry of 'building', which was so often chosen by the male-humans back in their community of Alfalfa; the building and fabrication of huts and tent homes, or the privileged spiral treehouse that her grandfather apparently had managed to carve out, and that no other underling in Alfalfa seemed to possess, strangely enough. The information she now heard was of a completely different order, and she just couldn't fathom how these towering Bastian homes were built, what kind of materials they were made of, and how they even came up with the idea of building them so very high up into the sky.

In any case, all this was as real as could be, because

the hologram told them about it with its enthusiastic, but sometimes cracking robotic voice, and the environment around them was the indisputable and irrefutable proof of it.

The self-thinking machinery, which was called computers, seemed to occupy a place in almost every home, and in almost every habitable space of these looming, towering structures. They were all connected to each other, and this form of machinery not only did most of the thinking for the Bastians, it also heated their homes, wherein they, after a long day out, sought refuge again. The hologram called all these things 'infrastructure,' together with the large network of railways resting on gigantic round stone poles on which also computer-controlled vehicles drove. These vehicles brought the Bastians in a targeted manner to their destinations, such as to their 'places of industry' where they usually, and better yet, as cheerfully as possible, had to appear again early in the next morning. Thomias thought it was all wonderful, nothing more than amazing, and when the third theme: 'artificial applications within nature' was being broached, he couldn't help but think that Star had also adjusted her opinion somewhat in the meantime. In any case, the hologram had changed appearance again, and now a characteristically looking scientist suddenly spoke. At least, a character like Thomias introduced and pictured himself, when he fancied himself an inventor, engineer, or scientist again.

The two Alfalfans were now very specifically and very methodically instructed within the ins and outs of this technological stronghold, and many a little hopping, and also snotty little Bastian had surely dropped out already. The hologram spoke to them on a somewhat academic level: 'Isn't man dependent on nature for his resources? Just take the large tree parks that can be found here and there within our majestic metropolis, for example. But make no mistake!

Most of these trees are made out of plastic, with a built-in mechanism that can reduce the CO_2 in the air and convert it into oxygen, just like a real tree would do. The only difference is that these dendrologic surrogates are very sustainable, don't wither away, and on top of that, don't leave their annoying mess on the ground. Star had to swallow a wad once again.

'And among these masterpieces, there are also trees that mainly extract CO_2 from the air and then store it in large underground reservoirs. CO_2, which can then be used on a large industrial scale. And even for the food industry, so that crops can grow more efficiently...' But Star shook her head firmly and believed she now had her second point of criticism about the operations within this city.

A so-called artificial plastic material that can extract this CO_2, this strange substance, from the air, and then use it again for growing crops?

According to Star, this could only mean one thing: that these vegetables would get a very nasty and also unhealthy plastic taste within their outcome, within their textures. But then again, who was she exactly? Some ordinary underling from the community of Alfalfa? A remote hamlet that these Bastians had probably never heard of before? Or simply just too insignificant for these technological thinkers? Nevertheless, one thing was very clear to her regarding this material: if this plastic was such a persistent substance and produced so many destructive by-products, why didn't they come up with a better alternative? Instead of getting rid of these annoying and wasteful by-products in a big roundabout way? In her view, it was like carrying water to the ocean. Could the majority of their high-quality inventions perhaps contain such a contradictory slant? That was certainly something to think about thoroughly, and in Star's case, perhaps even major point of criticism number two; a view with which she could now summarize this entire technological society. However, she kept her mouth shut towards Thomias, and certainly towards the occasional Bastian, whom they, in the meanwhile, had briefly spoken during their trip. Because, the two were still guests in this place, and if one thing wasn't to be called decent, it was to offend the host, no matter how much one might disagree with him...

The lessons of the hologram were now almost at its end, and the imagery therefore pointed them towards another facility, if they felt a need to learn more about Bastion's vision on the human body and its health. But just before the hologram would disappear again, he told them briefly about the developments of this society that were still in full swing. After all, the possibilities were literally limitless, and this talking device therefore gave them the example that one day they would even possess their own climate, while being able to regulate it at the same time. Such as cloud factories, that would provide them with plenty of water and also protection from the sun. It was now Star who pulled Thomias by the lapels of his vest, while dragging him towards a facility that had apparently expanded very fast lately, by offering the Bastians a free and complete body scan. They were able to join a group of students who happened to be on a study trip to this facility, and again no one seemed to turn around or look up when the two Alfalfans joined them in their midst. The Bastian youth was used to such eccentrics, were ultimately quite easy-going in that respect, and the only thing that a single student or older visitor to this building may have thought when eying these two oddballs was the following: you see, everyone turns around eventually...

'It's really nothing more than a logical approach of the human body,' was what the tour guide said.

'...Nevertheless, a practice that has made this entire facility to what it is today.'

One of the students lay down on a shiny white plateau, and a lucid cylinder of light began to rotate around the girl's body with humming sounds.

A geometric shape that Thomias recognized from the tubular pipes back in their own dome, next to the large gate, and protruding from the sides, while some already disappeared into the ground underneath, and that the friendly guide from Meriva called an irrigation system. And a light form somewhat similar to, and as transparent as, the speaking holograms that, with intervals, appeared in front of them, sometimes slightly flickered, and sometimes disappeared again for a few seconds. A biological-statistical make-up of the girl's body soon became visible on an electronic display, and the tour guide pointed the information out with some enthusiasm: 'A total body scan...' she said. 'Isn't it wonderful? Deviations of the body are immediately demonstrated in this way, for which suitable solutions

154

are then offered. The state of blood cells and oxygen levels, DNA make-up, BMI, and even one's personal lifestyle; everything is taken into account to point out whether a potential bodily weakness is lurking somewhere... But!' the woman stated enthusiastically again. 'Not before one has looked at one's own energy field, of course, at one's own radiation, at one's own electromagnetism, and that's what the primal people used to call aura back in the day, if I'm not mistaken. Because, and even though it can't be observed with the naked eye, it still hangs around all of us, and from that alone one can obtain very valuable information of one's own constitution...'

Thomias wanted to jump for joy by hearing this. 'You see, Star?! You see?! Technology! You can do all sorts of things with it!' But the group of students looked at him somewhat angrily. Because, silence had to be offered at all times, certainly in a public building, and especially during an important lecture like this one. Star, in turn, had her reservations once again. Because, all this might have been nice to hear and all, perhaps even to be called profoundly inventive, what she started to notice was that here in Bastion they only seemed to intervene at moments when things were almost, or already, too late.

And even though a full body scan could certainly be called preventive, it was often only used when a Bastian started to notice obvious health problems.

In Meriva they seemed to tackle this aspect more specifically, more directly, and much sooner, simply by offering their inhabitants crops that were naturally, and biochemically, intended for the human species in essence. There were simply no serious or persistent diseases there, because these were suppressed in advance by the nutrients of their crops. And if one did catch a cold, or even worse, then it could be attributed to a reduced resistance, and then the own immune system would eventually act as a healer. Star weighed all these things against each other somewhat: the pros and also cons of such workings in Meriva, and of course, those that were practiced in Bastion. And even though she already knew where her preference lay, she couldn't help but notice a certain despondency within herself; a certain dispiritedness because she very well realized that a community like that of Meriva, as serene as could be, and with whatever good intentions behind it, simply just couldn't catch up with the developmental growth as Bastion was currently making. This immense city simply had far more knowledge at its disposal, and therefore also more power. It seemed to be swimming in its own currency, and they also had, and that roughly estimated, about a thousand times more civilians.

Star and Thomias didn't know much about the clash between these two societies, or about the finer details of their disputes, but perhaps they would find out soon? For now, however, they had gained enough knowledge and inspiration from these surroundings. They now both had a more global picture of this metropolis, and of its inhabitants, and perhaps another time they could enter into conclave about it with the grandmaster of Meriva. And perhaps, just perhaps, they could then find out what was actually going on between these two societies; and why such a small community as Meriva dared to take on such a great force of power; against such a gigantic and also massive technological stronghold as Bastion was, and why their own small natural society was perceived as a threat to this grandiose vestibule in the first place… And even though the grandmaster had already told them a thing or two; told them about the domes that were predominately dominated by her wise men, by their elders, and that they stood in contact with each other, and that they perhaps even received orders from the bigwigs here in Bastion, Star still very much wanted to sit down with this grandmaster again to see if they could come up with some sort of plan; just some easy-going mutual rendezvous between these two societies that could eventually, and perhaps, even lead to a real peace resolution; to a form of mutual understanding. Something had to be found in this city that could rekindle the apparent icy connection between the two superpowers, and their citizens. But she also knew that this ideal picture would be far from easy to achieve, and perhaps even impossible to establish. She absolutely had to see this grandmaster again, but, and of course, there was also a downside to that scenario. Because, would they be welcomed in that valley again in the first place? And, would this grandmaster even want to see them again? Star straightened her shoulders. That scenario was for a later concern… For now, they still had some currency in their pockets, and a few days to kill, and this time they decided to just walk around aimlessly; just to see if anything spontaneous or interesting would occur. Just talking to some Bastians here and there; just as they'd done so at the beginning of their visit to this stronghold.

It did the two good to see that there were still some groups of Bastians who maintained some old traditions, apparently…

Star and Thomias walked somewhere in a suburb of Bastion; there where high-rise buildings were frequently alternated with lower forms of architecture. They walked under high railways, where vehicles drove over their heads with breakneck speed, and also with that characteristic low-produced humming sound. And as quickly as these vehicles moved, as slowly they toned down this acceleration when their sensitive sensors noticed an exact same stretched electric vehicle approaching in front of them. Nevertheless, this entire district; the district that Star and Thomias now walked through, struck them as somewhat backward, and perhaps even poor. More clutter lay around than anywhere else in Bastion. The buildings were less well-maintained, and the high, overarching rail network seemed to offer a certain shelter to the many Bastians who apparently had trouble keeping up with the times, with the pressure, and with the progress that dominated in other sections of this metropolis. Because of the high rails- network towering over their heads, and which managed to cast a large shadow over this section of Bastion, Star felt like being enclosed again; enclosed again inside a dome in which her community Alfalfa was also locked up, and this seemed to leave a sour aftertaste in her mouth. Alfalfa... How would Grandpa Maxwell actually fare by now? Would he have picked up his daily life again? Or would he slowly, but gradually, waste away from grief over the loss of his precious Star? While one of the elders stood paternalistically over him, because of a runaway underling who also happened to be his granddaughter? Star had no idea of course, this was all guesswork, and she didn't really wanted to know either. She felt a certain regret towards the man of course, and also a form of anxiety crept up within, but she absolutely didn't regret one thing: because, no matter how many underlings might suffer from this rebellious escapade, Star just had to choose for herself...

It did the two good to see...

Not the somewhat dilapidated houses, the many rubbish and newspapers lying scattered around, and that the wind sometimes eagerly managed to play with, or the handful of Bastians who seemed to linger in their personal misery. No, it did the two good to see that in a place like this, old traditions were still being upheld. Just a place where some human contact was still possible, and that in combination with a barter of one of the first primary necessities: the food that mother nature non-stop produced and that a handful of Bastians still seemed to appreciate, fortunately. The two Alfalfan visitors wanted to know more about this hustle and bustle actually, and they decided to talk to one of the market vendors; just to gauge what his vision was on this whole food business precisely. But the man, with his thick black moustache, and a flat cap on his rounded head, shrugged his shoulders somewhat indifferently. 'It is what it is,' was what the man briefly and concisely said. But Thomias and especially Star had hoped that this man would tell them his overarching vision; his view on the fundamental differences between the artificial food products that were so wholeheartedly recommended in the society of Bastion, and the products that he himself sold: the more organic and reasonably biological ones. And also what visible effects these had on the Bastians and their health, and which edible products they themselves preferred the most, if they would have the say...

But the man didn't have an immediate answer to these questions, and perhaps they were a bit too complicated for him, a bit too broadly oriented, so to say. Nevertheless, the man came across as a reasonable guy, and he told the two exactly how things went down, exactly as he had always experienced them himself, and not an ounce less or more…

'We are just ordinary market traders,' was what he said. 'We buy our vegetables from an illegal wholesaler and then sell them on for a little bit of profit. The worst parts are usually left over, and at the end of the day, we take them back home with us, or we give them away to the poor wretches, the poor souls that you've probably already seen lying around in their tents and self-made shelters. In this way, we can still make some form of a living, right? And even though what we're doing here isn't entirely allowed, it's nevertheless still somewhat condoned. There has to be some kind of underclass within this society apparently, and the upper echelon isn't very fond of people rioting or rebelling, so they just let us be. But the 'normal' people, and the man made a joking hand gesture, '…they don't visit here. The majority of these ordinary people buy their food in online stores, because that's where the products are being scanned. A certain scanning is also often done of people themselves, so that the buyer immediately can see which is the strongest crop to buy and consume.

In that way, people pay currency according to nutritional value, so to speak, and all of this is, of course, arranged via the large interconnected computer network, or as we call it here, 'the net.' And since the average Bastian is constantly busy with coping with everyday life, while keeping their heads afloat as good as possible, these ordered food parcels via the net are also brought into people's homes, even when they aren't home themselves; via specially designed shafts. But not before such a particular parcel is thoroughly scanned of course, and before it is taken up by the designated residence. This little trick is constantly evolving and being tweaked, and it seems to work more efficiently and more productively by the year. At the very first introduction of this production process, only shapes and contours within the parcel were being checked. And sometimes bananas were seen as a firearm for example, together with some other dubiously shaped crops. But nowadays this whole production—and delivery process is much more refined and advanced. And about that banana issue, we are talking about at least fifteen years ago here… Eating out is already a luxury for many for example, and that is mainly and exclusively done by the bigwigs, by the big shots, and by the exuberant wealthy within this society, because, for the average citizen, it has almost become unaffordable nowadays. And since the beginning of this year, it has even become somewhat fashionable to eat old and classical food, among a growing group of Bastians. Old, in the sense, food which is collected outside the walls of Bastion. You know, slimy vegetables and such. What are those things called again? Oh yes! Okra!' The market trader looked at his colleague with a laugh and jokingly put up a nasty face, and Star did the same with Thomias.

'Well…' continued the vendor. 'It's apparently a niche…'

Thomias thanked the man with enthusiasm for his, in the end, fascinating story, and he bought a small bag of fruit for the journey underway, out of a sense of gratitude. And even though Star wasn't to happy with this, she understood Thomias' intentions. Nevertheless, if the two wanted to stay a little longer in this technological stronghold, then they had to find a way to scrape up some extra currency. Star therefore, and somewhat boldly, walked up to a random merchant and asked him if he might be interested in some 'antique stuff.' And the man certainly was. And when he saw the piece of fool's gold with flint pass by, or Star's extra clean shirt that she hadn't put under her vest for all that time, and which Thomias had forgotten she carried with her in her pouch. Or when this vendor saw how Thomias shot some small pebbles around with his small self-fabricated catapult, the merchant was wildly enthusiastic and already sold.

'Fantastic!' the man exclaimed. 'Nothing more than fantastic! Indeed, beautiful antiques! I can definitely find a market for these kinds of objects!' And with currency signs in his eyes he turned to his new acquisitions, completely forgetting about the two Alfalfan sellers, who were still standing in front of him.

It was a lovely day today. They had enough currency for some extra food, and at least two more nights of shelter right now, and with that in mind, there was nothing left to do but relax, while a beautiful, bright afternoon sun shone on Bastion, bathing its high towering structures in yellowing tones of light, while leaving playful streaks of shadow on their sides.

A Good Conversation

The two friends walked through many neighborhoods in a relaxed manner, and eventually, along wide water canals that together carried their streams deeper into the city. The sun had lessened its sharpness in the meantime, while it shone calmly and without imposing itself, on the quietly flowing bundles of water around them. The reflection of light particles on the water made these wide canal quays for even bathe in a warm orange glow.

And even though not a single soul seemed to be around, Star thought she had noticed something further on; a black silhouette in the distance that stood out against the full light of the sun. She quickly tapped Thomias on the shoulder, who was scanning the waterflow below him for any form of life, when she pointed towards the small black figure that was sitting there, half bent at the canal quay. Thomias nodded, and they decided to take a look.

The small dark silhouette turned out to be an elderly man; an older man who spent the remains of his days mainly fishing. The man liked to be by himself, so he said, and Star immediately and silently wondered whether a busy life like that of the Bastians became less and less attractive as one got older, and if that was perhaps the reason why the man isolated himself so much and so often; there on the edge of the technological fortress called Bastion, cut off from its ongoing and never-ending imposing pressure tactics. In any case, Star would surely find out. But to become so personal right away, without even having introduced themselves first, was even for her bold character an a bit too cheeky approach, probably not that smart to do, and it might shut the man even more down.

In any case, the old man had set out his course again, and seemed to accept the sudden appearance of these two eccentrics. And who knows? A not too complicated, and also unbound conversation, might be nice again for a change.

And he explained his fishing method to these two unorthodox characters, who were eyeballing him with their somewhat strange gaze. The man told them that he had always fished in this way and didn't know any better; by means of a wire with a small mechanism and sensor attached to it, so that, if a fish dared to come close to this hypermodern lure, it would send out a small shockwave, measured to the size of the particular fish, and once this fish was stunned, the old fisherman could easily haul it in with his large fishing net.

The man smiled briefly at Thomias as if this fishing-gadget was the most normal thing in the world, but instead of Thomias returning the friendly gesture, he picked up a large stone that had crumbled from the stone embankment, and then threw it into the water in a frustrated way, while the old man looked at his action suspiciously. Was this young man disturbing his waters all of a sudden?

'That's just great!' exclaimed Thomias, pulling his hair in desperation.

'Inventions! Some huge! Many big! And countless

other ones, smaller! They just keep popping up in this place! One after the other! How am I ever supposed to move within such inventors' circles now?! I'm so terribly behind! Soon, everything will have been invented, and I'll just be that big-mouthed and bragging man-boy who can't even show one invention; not one discovery that could distinguish me from the rest somehow… Thomias sat down on the quayside, defeated of course, and while dangling his legs down, he stared with frustration at the dark water below him through which he couldn't even see anything. This realization seemed somewhat synonymous to his life. He thought he was a great inventor, or at least carried that capacity and ambition within him, but he just couldn't manage to put it into fruition. He literally and figuratively, just couldn't see through that dark turbidity below him. Beneath that annoying, impenetrable, opaque barrier. Past those countless small particles of water and of the sediment lying even more below, and that prevented him from seizing that luminous bundle of discoveries and progressive ideas that had to lie buried underneath there somewhere.

'I'm glad that I got rid of that ridiculous catapult!' he sulkily said to himself, and to anyone else who wanted to listen. 'It was nothing more than a lousy and stupid invention to begin with!' And even though Star understood his inner turmoil all too well, for now it was perhaps better to let him cool off somewhat, there on that refreshing waterfront. It'll be okay Thomias, was what she thought to him. And even though that weapon of yours might not be a great invention, I still have the feeling that this concept might work to our advantage one day. And Star, and without fully realizing it, was indeed right at that moment, because that peculiar little V-shaped wooden weaponry might become much handier than she thought, even much more suitable than Star could have imagined in advance…

Star decided to ask the man a few questions before leaving him alone; before letting him enjoy his old age and leisure time again. She had already introduced herself to him, and now she decided to ask one of her own pressing questions; questions that had been burning on her lips for a little while now. She asked the old man point-blank if he knew of the community of Meriva, and if he'd ever heard of it, but the man initially reacted somewhat distant to her questions.

First that mischievous boy who chased away his fish with his clumsy behavior, and now this girl asking him about something that the Bastians normally didn't prefer to talk about? An unwritten rule within this society that she, as a presumable Bastian, surely must've known of? He attributed this rudeness to a form of youthful rebelliousness and carelessness nevertheless; a certain naïve audacity that he had also carried within himself in his earlier days. The man thought for a moment with his head full of gray hair, with his somewhat hunched back, and with his bony limbs. Perhaps he could now, and in turn, teach the youth something about his accumulated knowledge? But the man also realized that he had but sparse information about this unknown community, that apparently lay not too far off from his own city; a society of presumable savages that had been getting in the way of the Bastians so annoyingly, and for so long by now. And so the man decided to just be honest about the matter.

'I don't know that much about that nature city, you

know. The only thing I do know, is that our government has been hunting it down for quite some time now, but I'm not sure why that is exactly…'

The man looked down at the water in a form of embarrassment it seemed, and Star thought she understood why. It was indeed a strange phenomenon to label a community like that of the hidden valley as your archenemy, but to know little to nothing about its people at the same time. Because, and according to Star at least, a lot of information could be deduced from that alone. Nevertheless, Star decided not to go that deep, and to keep things a little more superficial. She then asked him if he wasn't curious about these people, and if he didn't wanted to know more about them, although the man claimed to feel nothing for this.

'They may not even be bad people,' the man said. 'But I know nothing about them. I don't speak their language. I don't know their customs. And most likely we have nothing in common. Besides… and as far as I know, we are on top on an intellectual level in this world, and that definitely goes for the field of science and technology, so I have no idea what I could possibly learn from them really…' But Star tried to explain that the materials the Merivians work with may be perceived as primitive, they nevertheless had made discoveries that sometimes even seemed to surpass the knowledge of the Bastians. And perhaps not so much in terms of technical aspects, but more in terms of an ingenious use of simplicity, and that combined with a certain effectiveness. Star swallowed a lump of despair down her throat again despite this, because she didn't know whether she should have said this to this man to begin with. Because, Meriva could indeed be labeled as completely insignificant, compared to everything they had seen in Bastion so far. She continued to believe in the power of the natural city nevertheless; in that of the hidden valley. There had to be a golden egg hidden somewhere there; something with which she could blow these Bastians away on an intellectual level. But what that should be, she had no clue of either. And shouldn't they have noticed that golden egg during their first tour through the valley already? Star had decided to rely on her intuition once again, and it had come out as a form of bluff presented to the old fisherman. The man had to laugh mockingly at what she had said. 'Well,' he said in turn. 'Name one mind-blowing invention that you've just uttered, and perhaps I'll believe you...'

Star looked at the slightly waving water stream for a moment, and at the fishing line that lay in that same water. She then looked at the old man, and followed the fishing line back into the murky water again. And Star told him that the Merivians also adapted their fishing techniques to the fish they were trying to catch. ' ... For example,' she said. 'There is a fish that they'd like to eat and that has a long row of serrated teeth ...' And according to Star, they caught this creature by using bait wrapped in a fine network of thin gauze so that the creature got its mouth and teeth stuck in it. After that, they'd only have to pull it on shore, with the fish still completely intact, and in perfect shape. 'One doesn't catch a fish any fresher...' she added with confidence. The man thought for a moment. 'Okay...' he said. 'That is indeed quite inventive, but also quite primitive, I'm not entirely convinced yet.' And Star decided to tell him a few more of such discoveries and inventions: the clever usage of their natural environment, and of course, and on top of it, the physical vegetable garden that their tour guide back in Meriva had told them so enigmatically of, and that Star was still very enthusiastic about. The man finally nodded in satisfaction, and said that he hadn't expected all of this. And in their shared enthusiasm he even added that he found it nothing but strange that some of these ideas and applications hadn't been implemented in Bastion yet, since they could've used some of them also, to a lesser or greater extent. Star agreed with this observation, but she was trying to find out why that was exactly, together with her still sulking partner. Nevertheless, she lied a bit by saying that they wanted to work all this out as a final assignment for the learning-bench…

'The learning-bench?' asked the old fisherman in surprise, and Star looked around with difficulty in her eyes. She seemed to have talked too much this time. How was she going to solve this? Thomias decided to come to her rescue.

He had already picked up a few things from their conversation, although he still looked at the two chatterers with a somewhat angry and frustrated face.

'Education!' was what she actually meant!' was what he shouted at the man; a term he'd learned earlier from one of the talking holograms.

'Oh, okay, okay,' said the man in turn. 'Has the youth found a new word for that term also?' And the man had to laugh as he pulled his line out of the water again, checked the small attached mechanism, and threw it back into the brown canal water with a splash.

Star thanked the man kindly for yet another exciting conversation, and then pulled Thomias by his ear because he really had to stop with this pessimism now. The old fisherman waved them a heartily goodbye, after which the man gradually became a small, dark silhouette again; outlined against the orange glow of the sun on the water and the quay around him; an ambiance that had only become fuller and more intense in color…

The Pool of Genes, The Talent Tree, and The House of the Ancestors

The two had been on a stroll for nearly two weeks by now, and even though Thomias was a little down in the dumps momentarily, Star could still say, and that with some sincerity, that she was quite proud of herself and of her nagging companion. The grandmaster of Meriva had accused them of a form of espionage, at least, he wasn't entirely able to place these two. Nevertheless, the two Alfalfans had gathered so much information about this city by now, that even the grandmaster had to be delighted in some way or form.

And if the leader of the hidden valley was willing to lend them a certain platform, then Star could make her findings known to him and his people.

And maybe, just maybe, something constructive could come out of all this? Provided that the grandmaster would let them back into his valley, of course. According to Star, there was only one possibility to do so, just one small opening, and that was to confront the Merivians with everything they had seen here in Bastion so far… With the last bit of currency the two had left in their pockets, they bought a bag of organic products from the market vendors, who in the meantime had become somewhat acquainted with the two. The two friends had stocked up their supplies, straightened their cotton collars once more, looked back at the imposing stronghold that still bore the name Bastion, and then set off again: for a two full days walk towards the natural city of Meriva that would hopefully welcome them with open arms, or at least, would grant them an entrance again…

The two managed to find their way to Meriva, and that without too much inconvenience. They had learned from their previous suffering; from wandering around in a dusty plain without food and water, and their plan for now was simple and clear: resting against the reasonably sheltered rock formations during the scorching sunlight, and building a campfire towards dusk with the dried out branches that lay scattered on the ground here and there, and then using those same sticks to roast the vegetables—that they earlier had bought from the market vendors—over that same campfire. And with the falling of dusk, and with that shining silver ball hanging high in the sky, to continue their steps in order to prevent loss of energy and dehydration. The two realized all too well that they had now exchanged the light for the darkness in their traveling to Meriva.

Or, and what they now also knew and realized, had turned daytime and nighttime around. And even though this felt especially unnatural in their particular case, it was, and at this moment, the most effective approach in traveling. And so it happened that after two full nights of walking, they had reached the cave entrance that would lead them back into the hidden valley; a valley that was no longer that 'hidden' for these two brave but also stubborn adventurers.

The Merivians seemed, and especially to Star's great surprise, actually quite happy to see them back as visitors, and perhaps it strengthened them in their belief that their natural society was worth returning to. And the sight of these two eccentrics perhaps also strengthened their belief that the Merivians weren't the only people in this world trying to find their way within a larger play of powers. In any case, the two were welcomed back in a friendly and hospitable manner, they were even called by their full names without any spelling mistakes, and they were escorted towards their spiritual leader in a respectful and also relaxed way... *That went perfectly!* thought Star to herself. *Even much better than expected!* And she couldn't wait to meet the grandmaster again.

Because, she at least, and she looked questioningly at Thomias, had a lot to tell him...

The grandmaster sat down in his chair: 'Well, let me hear what you have to say then.' But the man also looked somewhat bored, as if this conversation would lead to nothing. Thomias looked at Star with frustration in turn, because, for the umpteenth time, he had nothing to say in these important conversations, had nothing to contribute, and he was slowly but gradually starting to despise himself for it. He had to leave this up to Star again, for the umpteenth time...

Star was eager to have her say on the other hand, and she told this leader in great detail about her findings. And even though she didn't really know where to begin with her story, she nevertheless decided to start at its core; with the inhabitants of the technological metropolis they'd just come from. The grandmaster kept his lips sealed and listened carefully. Star told the man that the Bastians may seem a bit superficial at first glance, and may move around a bit statically, they turn out to be highly intelligent, and also open to reason in a closer conversation. And even though Bastion may seem like a very well-organized community, its inhabitants, on the other hand, seem anything but problem-free. And Star decided to point out a few things, including, for example, the disagreement about the number of possessions a person was allowed to have, but also the many strange health problems that caused these Bastians suffering, and that were often treated with strange medicines that at first glance didn't always seem to work. She also spoke with flair about the many progressive ideas and technologies that were flourishing in this technological stronghold. Because, this huge city wasn't only a vast pool of sorrow, as the grandmaster had once made it out to be, and Star also thought she could draw a small conclusion from the seemingly smoldering feud that had been raging on between these two communities for so long by now. In other words: the Bastians thought of Meriva in the exact same way as the Merivians thought about Bastion…

The grandmaster nodded along at Star's spoken words, but instead of being delighted with this information, his facial expressions, and that to Star's surprise, only became more serious and depressed. The man finally raised his hand in the air, which made Star stop speaking. He cleared his throat to get his vocal cords in order—which told Star that her story, in some way, had appealed to him—and then looked at her with a sad face.

'Have you shown them your necklace yet?' And Star placed her hand on her breastbone again, as she had done so often in her life. The pendant... Gosh... Completely forgotten about it... 'No...' was what she answered.

The man rubbed over his chin and then stared into nothingness for a moment.

'Peculiar...' he said. 'Very peculiar...'

But what was so special about that little wooden pendant she always carried around her neck, anyway?

A mysterious veil always seemed to hang over it. Because, showing the pendant in plain sight was definitely out of the question; here in the hidden valley, back in Alfalfa, and seemingly also so in Bastion. But the few who did get to see it, reacted so strangely to the small hanger, that Star was almost immediately forced to put it away again. As if the sight of it had to remain hidden, and the spiritual leader sitting opposed to her, also made it very clear that he didn't want to talk about it, let alone see this strange pendant again. Nevertheless, the grandmaster wasn't of the worst kind. Because, even though he could behave somewhat trivially sometimes, sometimes even losing his leadership allure for a moment, this man also didn't seem to be who he was entirely. Or, at least, didn't entirely made clear what thoughts occupied his mind exactly. Perhaps he was just messing about, perhaps he was very subtle in this,

but be that as it may, he had a knack for tagging these two people along in his own playful way, and through the many layers of knowledge that thrived within Meriva; tagging them along within their insights and ways of living. Contrary to this, Star still couldn't fully appreciate this man's behaviorisms, and this began to irritate her more and more. Because, he too seemed to be a person who was hard to reconcile with, who seemed to withhold certain crucial information, and who tossed up presumable mysteries that, according to Star, didn't have to be there in the first place. But this grandmaster, this spiritual leader of the hidden valley, wasn't born yesterday either, and he therefore realized very well that he owed these two teenagers some sort of explanation. He had once again granted the two access to this valley, and that had its reasons of course …

'Look,' said the man. 'I can remember our first meeting very well, and also your personal belongings, tucked away within your leather pouches, in which I took the liberty of sniffing through,' and the man looked briefly at Thomias.

'Your little weaponry, for example, can you tell me a little more about it in broad strokes…?' But Thomias had been in a depressive mood for at least three days now, partly due to that retarded catapult he had once fabricated, and now this failure of an invention was the first thing he had to speak about with someone?! He told the man, in a cynical way of course, that he once had the dream of inventing things, of becoming an inventor, of being able to explain the workings of movement in things and objects, but the only thing he could come up with was a V-shaped piece of wood with a slack cord of rubber stretched in between. The grandmaster wanted to interrupt him, because he already had the notion where this monologue was going, but now it was Thomias who raised his hand in a didactic manner. His tone became even more bitter, and the man decided to commit himself to this dreadful litany, and also to suffer through it...

Thomias also said that he, and not so long ago, even pretended to have a fraction of the cosmos stuck in his head, only by coming across an interesting little book found in some backward 'hall of knowledge.' He was a fool, a dunce, nothing more than a ridiculous wanderer, who had just learned the difference between daytime and nightfall, and still confused the fiery sun with the silvery moon sometimes. He was small, insignificant, and also to be called miserable, and he felt an animosity for anyone who had found their place in this world, and who felt a certain peace for it. He! On the other hand. And he pressed his index finger on his chest in a childish and theatrical way, was cursed, in any case. There was no honor to be gained from him anymore, and from now on he wanted to be left alone. By everyone! He turned his back to both Star and the grandmaster, folded his arms tightly, and then refused to do any more speaking.

Star looked at Thomias' back with a grin and then looked at the grandmaster with raised eyebrows; which said the man that this scenario wasn't all that bad, and this young man would surely turn around again soon, literally and figuratively speaking...

'Well,' said the man. 'I have no idea what has transpired there in Bastion, or between you two, but I don't think I want to know regardless. I didn't mean that much with my question about his so-called catapult, the only thing I was trying to indicate is that technology, or the urge to discover and invent things, will always try to impose itself on an individual in some way or form. And that's apparently also the case with him; a curiosity phenomenon that can't be entirely stopped. Nevertheless, we as Merivians believe that major developments like such should always be approached and handled with caution. Look, we don't claim the ultimate truth in this place, but we do know that we have a very fundamental approach in our possession; a certain essential truth that has been doing all the hard labor for us humans, and that for a very long time; for tens of thousands of years, for many millennia, and which lets us live in total harmony with our environment. And with the constant advancing technological progress of Bastion, there is no other way than to adapt to their development somewhat, but it will have to be in synergy with our own life's visions: visions and insights that we know are good because we haven't created them ourselves, and which have managed to touch this society as a whole and our own souls within. And the most ideal picture according to us would be: a harmonious living environment in which that which has created itself, and that which we ourselves have managed to create, merge with one another in harmony and synergy. And that which we as humans have created, made, produced, and invented, can only influence us in a positive, upward way. It all sounds very simple and logical, and basically it also is.

And that, in a nutshell, is what we have tried to suggest, and made very clear to the Bastians all this time. Even when they hunted us down, killed us, and put us into domes... But their ignorance, their arrogance, or their ego, or whatever you want to call it, seems to have really exceeded their intellectual capacities up to this point. They don't want to recognize our way of living at all, even detest it, let alone want to implement it into theirs. So, where we are now, is a constant fighting and defending to protect ourselves, together with the last bit of crucial knowledge we still have in our possession. But nowadays we have even fewer prospects, and not even a small sparkle of hope left. The only thing left for us to do now, is prepare ourselves to the fullest, for what could well become a second great war; a pandemonium that could wipe out almost everything; including the last remnants of flora and fauna that this world still holds in its possession...'

And even though Star may have lost some sympathy for this man at the beginning of their conversation, he had now won it back completely, if not more. On the other hand, Star couldn't help but think that this man, how wise he might pretend to be, was nevertheless driven by a certain form of paranoia. But hey... was what she also thought, perhaps that was the price someone had to pay to be able to call himself the leader of a certain community? No matter how big or small it might be? The elders in the dome were clearly guilty of it, the leader of the splinter movement could be accused of it, this great spiritual leader of Meriva as well, and undoubtedly also the greater powers that must be hiding somewhere high up in Bastion; those who were at the helm there, whoever they might be... *Paranoia...* that was the right word for now. Was that what seemed to torment everyone at the moment? Was it a certain means of power that was being upheld? Used for malicious purposes? Star couldn't quite put her finger on it in any case, didn't really know where all this was coming from, although she had the intuitive impression that she wasn't far off from the truth. *Paranoia... Where could the source of it lie?* She had no clue yet, but for now, it might be better to listen to the words of the grandmaster. The man rose from his wooden chair: 'But!' he said. 'Fortunately, it hasn't come to that yet! And even though I act a bit annoyed or distant sometimes, I would like to add that I find you two a very special lot. And that's why I've decided to initiate you further into the teachings of us Merivians. Tomorrow, one of my best guides will be ready to take you along, and educate you further. And as soon as that's done, I would gladly hear about your thoughts and findings. Because, even if you are spies...' And the man leaned forward in a dominant manner, '...then you can tell those at the helm of Bastion all about our wonderful visions and insights.'

And the man gave the two one of his characteristic winks again. 'Perhaps that will moderate their tone a bit...' The next morning, and exactly as the leader had promised, one of his best guides stood indeed ready. The man walked up to the two Alfalfans and greeted them in a friendly manner.

'Star! Thomias! Great to see you again!'

But those Merivians were a bunch of jokers, together with their spiritual leader. The grandmaster would appoint one of his best guides to them? The leader only had one! And that was really this man here; the guide who had called himself the best of both worlds during their first meeting, and also during their very first tour. Star had to chuckle about it, although it worried her at the same time.

Because, if the Merivians had a knack for dealing with delicate stuff in this manner, and often went bragging and boasting over such important matters, they would have a very tough job of convincing Bastion, and its two million citizens.

The Merivians had to come up with something really good, and that very fast too! But Star's prayers, if they even could be called in that way, would be answered much quicker than she could've imagined herself...

The friendly, and also very sympathetic guide, walked ahead of them again; exactly as he had done so during their first tour, which created a certain déjà vu feeling amongst the three. And even though it hadn't been that long ago since that tour, perhaps about six weeks ago that they had walked through the illustrious physical vegetable garden, it felt as if these two Alfalfans had grown tremendously within their personal development in the meantime. And especially Star got the idea that her old life, her old familiar plant world, was increasingly being pushed into the background.

It seemed as if her grandfather, the elders within the communities, the members of the splinter movement, all these factors within her life's quest, became more and more insignificant, and less and less of importance. Almost as if she had transcended these factors in some way, had entered an entirely new universe, was gradually uncovering the problems of this newly discovered universe, and had now landed in the midst of a higher plane. She increasingly got the feeling that she had to do something important, but what that should be exactly remained cloaked in shadows. Nevertheless, despite all their setbacks, despite their constant wandering through newly discovered landscapes and surroundings, she still had the notion that she was being pushed in the right direction. A certain direction that gave both her and Thomias the idea that they held this newly discovered universe a bit in the palm of their hands; in the grips of two young people who, and that only six months ago, were still doubting whether their chosen industry was the right one for them...

'Look, Star,' said the cheerful guide. 'Just because you come from a dome originally, doesn't mean you don't have the potential to gain knowledge for yourselves. On the contrary... From our first meeting, I could detect a certain wisdom behind that gaze of yours, and that's why I want to take you, as well as the polite Thomias, to the house of the ancestors. Because, I'm almost certain that people like you will be open to it...'

The three hikers walked some more through the hidden valley, walked past the physical vegetable garden, and then entered a beautiful cave where only the dripping of water was audible, and where reflections of sunlight were outlined on the uneven rock formations that surrounded them. The guide stopped at a large stone plateau with a large hole in the middle, in which a bright shining pool of the clearest water the two had ever seen, lay. In front of this hole lay a large piece of parchment spread out; with unknown writings depicted on it. The guide suddenly, and without asking her beforehand, pulled a thin flaxen hair from Star's forearm and then threw it casually into the shallow pool of water. He looked at it with fascination and then wrote some strange characters on the piece of unrolled parchment; something he had undoubtedly done before, given the thickness of the scroll. The man then addressed the two, without looking up from the pool of water, or looking up from the scripture.

'Look,' he said again. 'It's not all that difficult, and actually quite logical.

In the house of the ancestors we dive into your gene pool. We dive into this little puddle here, and we look at the many embodiments; we observe the many family ties with which you've shared a blood bond. We look at the many weaknesses and also many strengths that have been built up over the course of years, centuries, and perhaps even millennia, and put them against one another. And if the procedures have been carried out correctly…' and the man still looked attentively into the pool of water. '…then an analysis will emerge from these particles and molecules, which you then can use within your personal acceleration-process through life. A process that, if all goes well, will be used in a positive way to shape your living environment; causing an upward spiral, so to say.' The man looked proudly at the two, while his hand blindly wrote further on the piece of parchment. 'We as Merivians have now reached a point in time where the trial-and-error system of constantly having to relearn old knowledge has come to a standstill. We have accumulated so many insights in the past that we largely can skip parts of this learning process by now.

In this way, we can develop ourselves in a much higher tempo on a spiritual level, and that with fewer and fewer resources; something we also strive to do to keep up with Bastion's own developments in certain areas…'

The man kept his eyes fixated on the piece of scroll. 'And that brings us to point number two! Because, even though free will, will always remain in force within our loving society, we also understand that, when push comes to shove, each of us feels a certain tendency to create; a process which can be accelerated by the talent tree; there where your stronger points, your talents, are located around the roots of the tree, and your weaker points around the fanning out branches. And perhaps you may think to yourself that it's somewhat superfluous to name these weaknesses, but we Merivians see that entirely different. Think, for example, of a weak seed falling from the fans of a tree, which blossoms over time, and then overgrows the entire trunk... Because... if you give these dormant talents the chance to develop further, they could very well contain very special effects; and they could well be able to grow out to be one of your biggest strengths in the end...

Take yourself for example, Star. Your intuition has always been labelled as something laughable, as something impulsive, as something that didn't do much more than get you in some type of trouble; causing certain types of problems.

On the other hand, it was that exact same intuition that sparked your urge for an inner, and not much later on, for an outward search. An ever-growing urge to learn more about your natural living environment. An urge to look beyond the built-up frameworks that deliberately wanted to put you in a mold, because they, and here it is again, intuitively hindered you in your own growth. And to make it even more interesting, I'd like to take a look with you at your own personal gene pool. I don't know you all that well, Star, and at first glance I have the faintest idea who your parents or ancestors might be, although this little body of water here tells me a whole other story. I now know you much better than you think, Star. Not because of the stories you've told me earlier in our steps, but because of this masterful liquid aid here, which is able to reveal your entire background to me. I can also see, and you mustn't be frightened by this, that your father had a natural predilection for biology, and especially for botany, and your mother... And the man leaned forward some more, now almost touching the water with his nose, as if he had to search very deep and very hard to be able to find something. 'And your mother...' he said again, although the man seemed to be startled all of a sudden.

Well, not necessarily startled, but his face seemed to distort, while looking inquisitively at Star for a moment.

The man then talked to her in a somewhat halting and softspoken voice: 'I can only tell you this, Star: that your father would have been very happy and also content with his life if it simply had remained as it was. But it seems that your mother had dragged him headlong into her enthusiastic, and also impulsive plans.

Very heroic plans, Star, don't get me wrong, but against an invisible enemy that was much, much more powerful, than she could have ever imagined. The people in her dome didn't want to believe her when she said that there was much more going on in their little world than they could ever realize, and that they had to rebel against this power, that they had to stand up against it.

Your father loved your mother dearly, but he also

cherished his own life, and I sense a certain bitterness coming from him, when I slide my hand over the gene pool. I can't tell you much more in detail, but what I do detect is a glimmer of hope, and I also sense that this man is highly pleased that he was able to pass on his book containing all the plant-data to you. Because… You see… Somehow, and intuitively, he just knew that he had to pass on this book to his unborn child. And that gives him, all the way up to this day, a great deal of joy, and also a great sense of pride. Simply, because you are his daughter, of his blood, and you and he share a lot of similarities…' Star wiped away several tears of course, and with those beautifully spoken words this exciting and eye-opening tour also came to an end…

Something Needs to be Done!

Thomias and Star had gradually become prominent figures within this society, and they didn't exactly know what they owed that honor to, but they certainly seemed to be treated in such a way. A grand plenary meeting was set up, and why so, and whether that had anything to do with their sudden reappearance, they didn't know either, but two seats had been reserved for them at this meeting, and the grandmaster insisted that they'd join in without any grumbling or struggling. Excited voices coming from the meeting room could already be heard from a distance, although these loudmouths quickly fell silent when Star and Thomias entered the room, and took their places on the only two seats that hadn't been occupied yet. Star took advantage of this moment to gaze over the shiny wooden conference table, and also past the many faces who had their eyes piercingly fixated on her. She counted at least twenty people, if not more, together with the grandmaster as the only real chairman of this gathering. The man tapped on the table with a small wooden hammer in order to get everyone's attention. It was dead silent by now, and the man demanded that the councilmembers would look at him, instead of Star, and the man quickly went through the items on the agenda. Or, at least, through the small piece of parchment that lay in front of him on the shiny wooden table. The meeting was now officially opened and everyone stood up to briefly introduce themselves. Star wasn't too far off with her earlier estimate, there were indeed twenty-three people sitting at this large oval table: a small number of women who had all acquired a certain prestige and influence within the hidden valley of Meriva. The sympathetic guide, who in his friendly manner had shown the two Alfalfans the way in this natural habitat, filled with his knowledge and expertise. And a larger group of stern-looking men who either held an administrative position, or seemed to have knowledge of something they themselves depicted as strategic warfare. Star and Thomias were about to introduce themselves, slightly stammering and with blushing cheeks, although, and fortunately for them, the grandmaster decided to do this for them. Most of the members had sat down again, and now only the two Alfalfans and the grandmaster stood in front of their seats. The man leaned slightly forward, pressed his hand palms on the oval table, and then addressed the small crowd: 'Prominent people within our beloved Meriva, and dear members of this gathering.

Hereby I would like to introduce you to these two dome residents, who bravely fled; Thomias and Star. These two, at first glance, ordinary-looking teenagers, about whom many stories have already circulated within our beloved community, and which continue to resonate over the vast fields and meadows of our valley. Without fully realizing it themselves, they have done some fieldwork for us by traveling to Bastion, while taking a good look around there. And even though we know Bastion and its inhabitants all too well by now, we ourselves, as familiar faces, as bigwigs of Meriva, haven't been able to visit that place for at least five whole years now. And maybe, just maybe, something of importance has changed there in the meantime, something that could be crucial for us to know. And if such isn't the case, if no major changes have been implemented on a social or economic level, then that's to be called in our favor. Let us listen to Star and Thomias for a moment, because, whatever the current situation might be, and on whatever side the coin may drop, I'm of the impression that it would be to our advantage to refresh our memory somewhat with their freshly acquired intel. So that it makes us realize again who it is exactly we've been fighting against for so long. Hopefully in such a way, that it can give the shadow that Bastion has become to us in the past five years, a clearer and more defined outline...' The grandmaster looked at the two younglings again. 'Please, sit down,' and he then turned to the rest of the group. 'And that brings us straight to agenda point number one: 'Important findings from outside.' 'A crucial point of discussion that we haven't had on the agenda for far too long unfortunately. At least, not since that scoundrel had the audacity to walk into our blessed valley so nonchalantly, while enriching us with his specialistic babbling and never-ending jokes.' And the grandmaster nodded and winked at his only trusted guide, who had to laugh just as loudly at this gesture.

'Dear Star,' he continued. 'Please tell us some of your findings and the things you have seen in Bastion. Perhaps there is something we have overlooked...'

And so it happened that Star started to tell... At first somewhat awkwardly and somewhat stammering and blushing, but not soon after more substantively and more quickly spoken. And she told these, for her mostly unknown Merivians, exactly what they had experienced in those two full, complete weeks. She told them about the technological civilization that they had witnessed, about its inhabitants, and even about the various holograms that they had spoken and listened to, and that had referred them to other interesting places. She also told these councilmembers, with a certain gravity and slight doubt in her voice, that she more or less thought about how things were faring with these Bastians on a social-emotional level. And even though Star realized all too well that it might be a bit premature to draw such heavy conclusions from just fourteen days of research, she nevertheless let her intuition do the talking again; her personal and character-bound strength that had never let her down up till now, and hopefully wouldn't do so today. Simply, because there was far too much at stake at this moment to come up with some errant allegations and mindless guessing.

Nevertheless, that was exactly what she was doing right now, and even though she realized this all too well, she confronted these prominent people without any hesitation about her findings on this interpersonal level. She addressed the members of this meeting with verve in her voice, and they all seemed to hang on her lips, and on every word that rolled out. Because, according to her, these people, these Bastians were, and as everyone knew by now, perhaps far ahead of their time in technological and scientific terms, they seemed to be quite underdeveloped in spiritual and intersocial means. And according to Star at least, it seemed as if they lagged behind in this because they had completely neglected those facets, solely focusing on their technological and scientific progress and developments.

Star was getting the hang of it, and the chairman motivated her to speak further if she felt the urge to add some more. Star thought for a second, although she wasn't entirely sure whether it would be the right thing to do to utter this new imposed insight. But the growing support of the grandmaster, and the surprisingly overwhelming feeling that this public speaking brought with it, made her decide to brazenly put on the scientist's hat. She then went on to talk about this alleged mental underdevelopment of the Bastians, and thought that it could be due to the following points:

One: the Bastians probably didn't experience this form of empathy during their upbringing. They seemed to live completely past one another, and were even encouraged to live their lives as solitary and as individual as possible.

And point two: due to their rapidly growing population and demography, and due to the related technological growth that they always had to catch up with and pursue, this human aspect of empathy and a feeling of societal cohesion had increasingly lagged behind, if there was still any present; simply, because this aspect became less and less of importance within their lifestyle, within their ways of living, and basically within their form of survival.

And point number three... And Star licked her index finger and then stuck it in the air like a real teacher would: 'And this is completely out of the blue, and an observation on my part... The possibility of spiritual expansion, which is flourishing so abundantly in your beautiful Meriva, is consciously being suppressed by the higher powers of Bastion...'

It was dead silent for now in the meeting room and the grandmaster believed he had heard enough.

'Thank you, Star,' was what he said. 'Thank you for these fascinating findings and your very clear explanation. You can sit down again if you want.'

But just as Star was about to do so, a man suddenly jumped up, and pointed in a warning manner towards the grandmaster.

'You see!' the man exclaimed angrily. 'Nothing has changed at all! Absolutely nothing! And the spiritual degeneration of the Bastians has probably only increased in the last years! I tell you! They don't care about us at all! Not even after our multiple attempts at negotiation! They are a bunch of snakes! And while we sit here debating like a herd of docile lambs, they just continue to spread this human decay from their poisonous glands, while they themselves keep hiding behind their impenetrable network of ever-deepening holes! I tell you!' And the man kept pointing angrily at his leader who could do nothing more but watch helplessly. 'We have to fight! Otherwise everything will be lost and for nothing!'

The grandmaster tapped his hammer furiously on the meeting table and the man, who most likely was in charge of the defense wing of Meriva, slammed his fist hard on the oval surface in turn, startling many other attendants of this meeting, after which he sat down in his chair again with a furious and distorted face. 'Let's keep this meeting as uniform and professional as possible, please!'

But the heated man mumbled to himself in such a way that it was still somewhat audible to the rest of the group: 'Yes…' he said in a soft but clear tone. 'We know these meetings by now…' And a dissatisfied commotion stirred in the meeting room... 'Okay,' said the grandmaster. 'If this is the prevailing view of many among us, then let's throw this whole meeting open right now.'

While he looked somewhat irritated at the previously heated man, who himself had calmed down a bit in the meantime.

'Let's just get straight to the last point, and let's start a dialogue about it.

I too am of the opinion that something needs to be done, and also very quickly, but it would be foolish to do so out of spite or on impulsiveness.

I understand your frustration and anger all too well, and it certainly has its core roots, but let's not cloud our minds with malevolent thoughts, because by now we know damn too well what happens when you confront evil with evil.

Moreover, it would be a shame to throw our years of preparations away unused, but that something needs to be done is without a doubt...'

The entire table fell silent again, yet, Star could hear the follow-up question to this statement from everyone's mind at the table. *Something had to be done... Indeed... But what exactly...?* Star looked at her buddy Thomias and he also seemed to be thinking hard and deeply about this huge dilemma. Nevertheless, a feeling of powerlessness prevailed once more. How could these two insignificant characters, without any knowledge of technology, without any knowledge of high-quality weaponry, and without even an army of hundred men behind them, ever take on such a boarded-up fortress as Bastion? Gosh, the two didn't even have anything they could call a home themselves. And even though they had become good friends with the Merivians by now, they probably would never lend them their meager army, no matter how thought-out or effective their proposed plans might be. Gosh, they didn't even have a plan at the moment. How could they ever pull this off? Would Meriva be nothing more than a hopeless patch of erosion in ten years' time? A piece of land that even the smallest of crawling creatures would turn their noses at? It would be nothing more than a shame, a pure waste of all such beauty. Was this then the ultimate result of a simmering feud between two parties who both refused to compromise? Star had always looked at life quite sunny. It was always her own living environment that managed to cast a cold shadow over it. But fortunately she had never really experienced a feeling of powerlessness, or feelings of completely losing hope. All this was simply too grand, too reach-less, for two ordinary people like themselves. Two young people who were still completely wet behind the ears in terms of political play, let alone being full-fledged diplomats. How could they, and that in the name of the great creative cosmos, ever conjure any ripples within this whole ordeal? They had the faintest idea, while the spiritual leader of Meriva was about to tell them even something greater: something they'd never even considered, and that would cause even more dents and cracks in the little hope they had left, if they had any; pushing them even further and deeper into that unknown abyss filled with sadness, sorrow and misfortune.

The grandmaster tapped his wooden hammer on

the oval conference table once more and then stood up. 'Before we start talking about a possible offensive, I first want to discuss something very crucial with you.'

And he looked at Star and Thomias again.

'You may have had the feeling of just wandering around somewhat aimlessly within our beloved Meriva, but I still want to point out, and I believe I'm speaking for all of us here, that we've enclosed you in our hearts by now, even if you are spies...' And the man gave them one of his characteristic winks again, which said Star that his previous form of suspicion was now really out of the window. 'And that's why I want to be completely open with you; by telling you one of our biggest reasons why we are so hesitant and reluctant about a possible peace treaty. At the same time, I also want to inform you about one of our highest insights that will keep you somewhat Merivian, should you ever decide to seek your salvation elsewhere. We realize all too well, just as you two did during your short visit to Bastion, that the Bastians are essentially the same as us. However, we Merivians hold a delicate form of knowledge in the palm of our hands that we can never just simply hand over. Not without a one hundred percent guarantee of trust. An insight that, if it were to fall into wrong hands, could completely disturb the balance of life and everything connected to it. That's why I won't explain it to you in full detail, because it's simply far too precarious for that...

I'm talking about the passage of souls here, and about our free will. Something, as you already have noticed, already has been severely restricted in this world.

And I'm talking about an eventual stopping of the flow of life, and thus also an ebbing away of all its lifeforce. This means, in a nutshell, although that may be said somewhat irreverently, that this dimension as we now know it, could be completely lost and who knows what else with it. Because, even if our own Merivian knowledge only touches the edges of this dimension, unfortunately, but perhaps also for the better, all this; this entire forced plan of Bastion, could make the entire so-called congregation of souls to a standstill. And so also make our chance for an ultimate merging with the higher divine; that which we call the ever- creative cosmos, disappear. And once that happens, it will mean that we will wander around forever within this dimension; within a technological network set up by the Bastians, which can't be escaped from, and which we may not consciously support at all, but which we have all unconsciously and somewhat willfully contributed to. And since our conscious and unconscious are part of all our previous lived lives, and ultimately also part of our free will, there is absolutely nothing that can be done about it anymore, and we are literally trapped within this dimension; both physically with our bodies, as well as spiritually with our minds and souls. And that! My dear Thomias and Star is exactly what we as free spirits, as freethinkers, and as protectors of this forest of life, are trying to prevent. The true answer to this cosmic question remains unclear to us, just like the outcome of the battle we are waging, but we believe it will not be long before this suffocating truth will reveal itself to us, and will arrive upon us. And until this doomsday scenario unfolds itself, we hope that the earth, its trees, and our hearts, will bow in mercy, so that we may have one more chance to shine in all of our glory...'

The grandmaster looked with seriousness at the man who earlier in the meeting had taken the right to speak out of turn, and with which he had managed to break open this entire meeting.

'I have to agree with you, lieutenant' was what the grandmaster said to him. 'A form of negotiation, in any form or shape, doesn't seem to be appropriate anymore. And as for fighting, the only thing we can do now is defending the narrow passage to our valley; something that's becoming increasingly difficult with our dwindling manpower, let alone launch an organized effective attack on Bastion, because that would be downright suicide. Then we might as well walk into their stronghold with our wrists already held together, politely asking them to put handcuffs around them… No…' And the man shook his head helplessly again. 'We don't stand a chance against their advanced weaponry and arsenal. Our population ratio was one to a thousand of theirs according to our latest reports, and that wedge between them and our demography has probably only increased with the passage of time. For every man we lose, they gain two hundred, if not more. Our attack would be nothing more than that of flies on a cow's tail. It's beginning to look hopeless by now. If they'd only understand, somewhere deep in their blunt minds, that if we were to join forces, we could evolve in all aspects of human existence…'

Star's Masterplan

That night, the two Alfalfans couldn't catch sleep at all. They understood the bigger picture a lot better by now, and the majority of the cards now indeed lay spread out before them on the imaginary table. With a few of the cards still closed, and among them a gloating joker who kept a tight grip on the reins, and knew exactly how to turn this all into a sickening game; a wicked game that Thomias and Star preferred not to have played, but they now forcefully had to, because they too, out of a form of curiosity, and also out of their own free will, had decided to join this table. Thomias therefore explored the most distant regions of his brain, to find a suitable solution for this dilemma, for this intense problem, for this impasse almost. But of course, the poor guy couldn't find anything suitable or substantial, and he once again looked sadly into the flaring and irregular flames of their small campfire. Star also thought hard of course, and also very deeply, although for now it was about completely different things. She could think of nothing else than her grandfather, and whether he also more or less knew about these pressing matters. She had to think of her parents, about whom it had always been said had died in some vague accident, and under strange circumstances. Star thought about the pendant dangling around her neck that, if seen by others, always made them shudder in fright, and that she, if to believe the words of her grandfather, had inherited from her own mother, if that wasn't yet another lie...

And she also had to think about her father's book that she had inherited from him; finally an answered question, acquired from the gene pool, which the guide of Meriva had told them so passionately about earlier on. Star couldn't help but think of one word; one term that the grandmaster had only mentioned about once, but kept stinging around in Star's head like a persistent, annoying, and also painful, cluster headache: *The shadow consulate...* Who were they exactly? And why did this grim term make herself shudder so? Was her grandfather perhaps part of it? No, she wasn't allowed to think that way. Did he perhaps have something to do with the sudden disappearance of her parents? Of his own daughter? No, she certainly couldn't think in that sense. Star quickly tried to sidetrack her thoughts by moving a log in the campfire, even though that didn't seem to help at all. All this was slowly starting to consume her, and the only thing she could do now, or so she thought, was still somewhat capable of doing, was to bite back somewhat. *But evil couldn't be confronted with evil, right?* as the grandmaster had so explicitly mentioned during the meeting, and Star finally thought what the man had meant by that. But a malignant tumor had to be cut away also, hadn't it? Before it had the chance to further spread through the affected body? Star grabbed her head in desperation, and Thomias simultaneously did the same without them having exchanged a single word about these difficult matters. *Rigorously cutting away... That wasn't nature's way, now was it? How could one get rid of something malicious without tackling it rigorously, and that without a scalpel, and without a firm hand...?*

Star thought deeply again, visualized this diseased

lump for a moment, and suddenly had an epiphany that instantly changed her entire mood.

'I've got it!' she excitedly shouted. And she looked at Thomias with a smile while he scratched his head in surprise. 'Thomias,' she said. 'What do you do when a small tree has a diseased branch?' And Thomias thought in turn. 'Well... then you cut it off, won't you?' he said, not quite knowing where Star was going with all this.

'Indeed!' Star excitedly exclaimed again, after she shook her head firmly. 'Or...?'

'Or what?!' exclaimed Thomias, irritated, not really in the mood to talk about plants, shrubs, flowers, trees, grass, or any kind of greenery at this crucial point. 'Or...' Star continued. 'Or you keep treating all the roots of the tree until the diseased branch shrivels, dies, and falls off by itself!' Star quickly stood up. 'I have to see the grandmaster!' But as Star was already walking away to do so, she was promptly stopped in her tracks, simply because Thomias halted her.

'Wait a moment Star, don't act so impulsively, please. It's already late, everyone has had a long day behind them, and some of us even had an exhausting meeting today. Whatever it is Star, whatever grand plan you are concocting now, it can probably wait. Meriva will still be here tomorrow, and Bastion most definitely will, if I understand the whole story correctly...' And Thomias had to chuckle at his own dryness, although he knew very well that this was not something to playfully joke about. Thomias decided to get some sleep, and Star followed his example. At least, she pretended to go to sleep, but instead she lay on her back and looked with wide awake eyes at the clear dark blue sky with its many constellations of stars that hung there for almost infinite miles high up in the air and that, if you looked at them long enough, and connected these sparkling dots together, even seemed to depict separate figures. Under the low snoring of Thomias, she thought about how to best tackle her idea, and while the twinkling abstract figures high up in the sky performed their dances, she drew a schematic plan in her mind. So that she could present it to the grandmaster the next morning, and as soon as the opportunity would arise. A man she now held in high esteem and who she now rightly could, and she probably could speak for Thomias as well, call their confidant…

At the first light of dawn, Star stood in front of the spiritual leader's room to present him her plan. And even though Star thought in advance that the man would be very pleased hearing about it; a tiny loophole within the net in which Bastion seemed to hold Meriva captive, this predicted outcome of hers was anything but the case.

'It could very well be that the soldiers will first open fire, and later on ask their questions. I believe it's too much of a risk…' was what the leader of Meriva said after hearing about her proposal. 'Certainly in those old and conspicuous rags you've been walking around in for so long by now. In addition, your so-called plan has to entail a lot more aspects; things you probably haven't even considered at all yet. Firstly, a self-assured attitude would be handy to walk around with, together with a substantive and quickness of tongue. Plus, you'll also need a proof of residence, a certain proof of citizenship, a visa.

Moreover, the Bastians see their own time as valuable, and their presence towards strangers from outside as a waste of time in general. As I've said before: this is a very risky undertaking... The Bastians hold completely different codes of conduct and standards, and some of them are even a mystery to us still. On top of that, if they find out that someone is moving illegally within their currency market, there is a big chance of years of imprisonment...' And the man looked with an unhappy face at Star, for purposefully burning down her plan, which had arisen from a constructive attempt at hope and certain recovery. Star looked angrily at the grandmaster, just as the lieutenant had done so during their important meeting yesterday. 'Well!' she said in a cynical tone. 'Then we might as well give up already, and dig our graves right now! Now, won't we?!' And the grandmaster watched her as she walked away with heavy steps.

'I don't know, Thomias,' said Star, when they sat around their communal campfire again that evening. 'I really don't know... Perhaps the grandmaster is indeed of the waiting kind? And all this time, he has been hoping that this ordeal might blow over by itself? Perhaps that was the real reason why that lieutenant guy reacted so fiercely during the meeting and verbally lashed out at him? Still, I can't wrap my head around it. I presented a reasonable plan to the man, and even if it comes down to nothing, it will give the Merivians at least a little hope for a while, and the Bastians hopefully a certain awareness...

I just don't understand it,' she said again, as she turned her face to the clear dark sky up above; searching for a ready-made answer that might flash by, shine by, or something of that kind.

'I really don't get it…' she said for the last time, after which she slowly but uneasily fell asleep…

The grandmaster understood very well that Star couldn't grasp the full picture, and he probably didn't quite get it himself either. Perhaps the setbacks that had followed each other in such rapid succession in recent years had made him fearful of some form of failure. And perhaps he, gradually but steadily, was beginning to doubt his own leadership qualities; pondering whether he shouldn't just resign from the high office he had held for so long by now. It could all have been the case, but whatever it was, it had given him the drive to carry out a plan once more; Star's plan, to be precise. And that next morning his faithful guide, who apparently also served as a messenger, stood in front of the pile of ashes where a small crackling campfire had stood burning the night before…

During the two months that followed, certain preparations were finally being made. Star had neatly worked out her plan on scraps of parchment, and the many appointed persons worked diligently on their tasks; without grumbling and without asking a single question about the how or the why.

And even Thomias applied himself zealously to his appointed task, even though he was now busy manufacturing and multiplying that which he had despised so greatly recently. Star, on her turn, was busy with nothing else but writing; writing, scribbling, and even more writing. And if she wasn't busy doing that, she held another piece of parchment in her hand to go over all the key points and to check whether they were still on schedule as a group. And so it finally came to a moment that to her, eight horses, four smaller ponies, sixteen large saddlebags filled with stuff and trinkets, and ten men of support were assigned, to be able to carry out her plan, and to accompany both her and Thomias during the exciting walk towards Bastion again. *May the cosmos protect them...* was what the grandmaster and many Merivian thought, when they saw the caravan depart...

The larger horses were positioned at a safe distance, a little outside of Bastion, and the heavy saddlebags were hoisted from their backs. Two men remained behind to take care of the horses in this inhospitable, barren landscape, which was no longer that foreign to them, to protect the animals from harm if necessary, and to guarantee the group a smooth and also safe journey back home. It must have been quite a sight from the outside; twelve men strong, including the two Alfalfans, carrying large saddlebags, this time hoisted onto their own backs, and with four small ponies at their sides, walking into this technological universe in an almost medieval manner. Many a Bastian looked up at the eccentric group, just as the Merivians themselves did when they saw the exceptional Bastian architecture protruding around them. And even though Star could understand their overwhelming impressions, and they were certainly appropriate at this particular moment, now was anything but the time for that. Star had foreseen that their group would draw attention to themselves in this way, so for now it was important to divide their limited time as efficiently and as effectively as possible. She therefore decided to briefly address the women and men in her ranks. To refresh their memories about the true purpose of their arrival in this place, after which they quickly continued their way.

A group of twelve who, even though they had put on clothing that made them somewhat less conspicuous, thanks to the advice of the grandmaster, still strongly stood out against the surrounding environment through which they were now walking. Star therefore decided to quicken their pace. At least, to the extent that was possible, with the heavy bags they were carrying around, in order to lead her group to a section of Bastion that seemed to belong to the underprivileged; there, under that safe high shelter of the wide but also dense network of rails, where automated electrical vehicles still constantly passed by with their low humming sounds. Star had a certain responsibility to bear now. Two certain responsibilities as a matter of fact: to carry out this plan that she had set up for herself, and secondly, to ensure the safety of her entourage as best as possible. And by returning to this part of Bastion, she basically killed two birds with one stone. Because, even though these dilapidated streets, of the apparent sinister characters that seemed to roam this section of the city, and of the somewhat despondent atmosphere that could scare off many an outsider, or a lighthearted Bastian for that matter, Star wasn't bothered by these factors at all. Star therefore walked comfortably towards the market vendor, who had to blink at least twice to recognize her. And although the man initially reacted somewhat reservedly to her proposal, he eventually agreed when he heard that he would receive a lion's share of the presumable profits.

'Okay,' the man finally said. 'Some of my men will be here tomorrow to help you further with your things.'

Star was very pleased with this promise of course, and since the word of a merchant could generally be labeled as trustworthy, she and her entourage finally decided to turn to the paupers with the question of whether they could use their improvised accommodations, perhaps.

The group of underprivileged Bastians made room at their burn barrels without grumbling or hesitation, which many a Merivian gratefully made use of by rubbing their hands to warm them by the flickering flames. And even though the group was somewhat tired from their three-day walking trip, an animated and reciprocal conversation seemed to develop in the midst of the large group, which only strengthened Star in the many suspicions she already had. But when the two large groups had gotten used to one another, even to such an extent that the group's shared energy itself almost became enthusiastic, this spontaneity seemed to change at once when an obscure-looking character decided to join in their midst, while carrying and introducing his own pitiful energy field to the prior spontaneous hubbub. Many a homeless person now walked away, who apparently didn't want to be associated with a person like this one. But Star, good-natured and spirited as she was, decided to tell this figure her story with some flair; in that way, trying to keep the now thinned-out group together. But this cloaked man, with his hood pulled far over his head, told her bluntly that her plan had no chance of success to begin with. Star looked at him in shock, at least to the extent it was possible, with the piece of cloth mysteriously concealing most of his face.

'Why not?!' asked Star, to get straight to the point,

and in that way also trying to mask her own growing doubt.

'You'll know soon enough!' shouted the man, who also could have been nothing more than an adolescent, while he walked away again; deep into the shadows that seemed to feed on this form of despair; a form of gloom that the mysterious figure had managed to display in a very short time, and also very effectively, and with which he, together with his sudden disappearance, also had taken a piece of Star's earlier self-confidence.

The first day of sales indeed proceeded with difficulty…

The many items were neatly displayed, the ponies stood ready to be ridden, and the now Merivian merchants were eagerly waiting to be of service and to welcome their first customers. But… not a single soul came to their party… And the only buyers that did show up, were the handful of Bastians who did their weekly market shopping at their regular Bastian supplier. This was to be called a real disappointment, and when Star and her team put their things away again at the end of the day, she assured them that the next day would definitely go better…

But the second day also went slowly, and even a little worse than the day before. Rain was pouring down from every side, despite the pseudo-covering of the rail network above them, and even the average customer had decided not to show up that day. Star scratched her nose a few times as she kept her eyes fixated on the high piles of parchment that now lay shielded under an orange plastic tarpaulin she had borrowed from one of the vendors; pieces of parchment that ultimately had to be her real trump card; her ace in the hole. Star found it ironic, but at the same time also somewhat bitter, that such potentially mind-expanding documents had to hide in the midst of heavy rainfall like this; in particular, in the midst of a dilapidated community like this one, where they figuratively could bring such beautiful weather…

Almost all the items were packed with some despondency again, except for some small figurines or handmade tools that were missing, because they had been sold to a random passer-by; to someone that looked at such an object as a nice knick-knack, something that was fun to give away, or looked nice on their dresser. Star once again spoke encouragingly to her group: 'Tomorrow will definitely go better! It has to be! I can just feel it! May the cosmos bring us nice weather!' And even though the weather had significantly cleared up during this third day of sales, it was also the saddest and most melancholic day the group had experienced so far. There were simply no customers showing up… Well, except for one insignificant customer who came to get a bunch of bananas to, as he put it himself, 'strengthen his body after a long night of drinking.' Star looked questioningly at the merchant who had helped her set this all up, although the man looked back at her with a shrug.

'Well, Star!' he shouted. 'Days like these also happen!'

The Merivian merchants packed their things even more dejectedly this time, while the Bastian vendors seemed to do so more cheerfully, since they could take their remaining goods and staple food home with them at least.

Star said nothing at all to her group that evening, and the newfangled Merivian merchants also didn't feel a desire or reason for any conversation, although the collective silence spoke for itself, of course. And in order to not create any false hope, Star decided to keep her mouth shut during that evening, although thinking about the following: *Tomorrow has to go better! I can just feel it! I promise!*

But during that fourth day, some Merivians began to complain.

'Give it one more day! Please! That's all I ask!' said Star somewhat hopelessly. But some of the Merivians saw the approaching storm already coming, even though it was only drizzling lightly that day, and the sun was showing itself around the corners so now and then.

'No one is showing up,' said a Merivian. 'And whether it's because there's no interest in our goods at all, or because we are in the wrong place, I can't tell, but this is starting to feel a bit pointless, and apparently it is becoming also...' And everyone, including Star and Thomias, was already busy dismantling their stalls in complete silence towards the end of the afternoon, when a large group of Bastians suddenly came walking around the corner...

A group of students, apparently, who seemed to be intrigued by all this stuff; picking at the remaining statues and figurines that still stood on display here and there, and who in all seriousness were wondering where they actually came from, and what origin they entailed. Despite this, only one Merivian could muster up the enthusiasm to tell this group about them; a group, apparently accompanied by a teacher. The Merivian merchant told them about the origins of these statues and figurines, about the deeper meaning behind them, and about the way in which they were fabricated. The rest of the Merivians simply continued packing their merchandise, while witnessing how a vibrant discussion began to stir among the cackling students.

'You see!' one of the students exclaimed. 'Real Merivians!' Exactly as I once learned in elementary school; nature people who use everything, that their biological environment offers them, at their disposal!

Not just that plastic rubbish that we get thrown at our heads every day!'

'Well, well,' said the teacher. 'That's about enough of that, okay?' And she turned to the Merivian vendor with a smile: 'That was a very interesting, and also very fascinating story, thank you for that. I'd like a few statues please, this one, that one, and that one also. And a staple of those, if possible. Real parchment was it…?! And the salesman nodded. 'Unbelievable… Exceptional! And I'd like a few of those writing tubes and quills as well.' And she turned to her group of students in the meantime. 'Tomorrow we'll be writing an essay by hand, in the good old-fashioned style and way. And I'm seriously wondering if you lot are still capable of doing so; writing legible markings on solid pieces of paper…' And the teacher had to chuckle to herself. She turned to the Merivian salesman again. 'By the way, will you guys still be here tomorrow?' And Star quickly looked up, dropped all her packing preparations in a hurry, and then swiftly ran to the group.

'We'll definitely be here again tomorrow! And you know what?!' she said with heavy breath. 'There will be much more to learn here! Here, you can learn just as much from us Merivians, as we could from you Bastians! Please, pass this point of sale along, next to this information I'm telling you! For anyone who wants to listen to it!' But the teacher had to laugh at these words, as she was handed her neatly wrapped purchased items by the Merivian vendor.

'Well...' she said, and that somewhat in surprise. 'I believe that already happened a few days ago...' And she called her group back together, after which they walked away, talking and arguing heatedly.

Star felt euphoric that evening, and the rest of the Merivian group felt that ecstasy also, although those feelings were perhaps somewhat misplaced.

This was indeed a strange turn of events, certainly, but Star decided to keep her mouth shut for the most part of that evening nevertheless, and the only thing she did say in a serious tone was the following: 'If tomorrow is another poor day, it will be our last day of sales, I promise you guys that.

If tomorrow is another meager day, we will pack up our things and head back home; back to our beloved Meriva. Because, if that will be the case, we have done our very best, but this all wasn't meant to be, apparently...'

The majority of Merivians were thrilled to hear this news, and instead of despondency, there was now a conviviality to be felt, and even some alcohol was served and consumed in the vicinity of the blazing burn barrels that could almost be called their own by now. But what

Star seemed to have forgotten in her early young life, was the wise life's lesson that good things came one's way if one knew how to behave humbly. And that one should never blow one's own trumpet too soon or too much, not even if it was born out of a form of youthful enthusiasm. But whatever it was, and whether all this was due to her perseverance and tenacity, she didn't quite know, but the next day was a day like the group hadn't experienced so far. The sun shone calmly right now, the humidity had been largely vaporized from the air, and many a group of schoolchildren and their supervisors walked up to Star's group with enthusiasm to see who these primitive people actually were; those so-called Merivians, and whether they indeed were related to the primitive people they had regularly learned and read about during their cultural anthropology lessons in college. Meanwhile, the Merivian sellers were doing their own thing, and even though they previously had their doubts about this whole endeavor, they now seemed almost addicted to all this selling of their wares, to the explaining about their culture, and to the mutual contact with these Bastians, who weren't that bad at all. And when even multiple groups of parents with their children in hand showed up, all circus broke loose.

Star figuratively slapped herself in the face a bit. *Dumb, dumb, dumb,* was what she sternly said to herself. Food! Completely forgotten about it… How nice would it have been to give these Bastians a taste, and also samples, of all the delicacies that were so frequently served in the hidden valley? Star tried to straighten and tighten this loosened stitch somewhat by teaching many a Bastian housewife, or at least, head of the household, with enthusiasm about the many Merivian spices and natural dyes that they could experiment with in their own kitchens. The many Merivian insights and short stories; all of which were transcribed by Star, and which she had reproduced so frequently and vigorously over the course of weeks, seemed to fly over the market counters faster and faster.

And the same went for the many fertility statues, the handmade utensils for handling flint, for the many stalled out beaded jewelry, and other Merivian haberdashery. And when the Bastian children finally noticed the catapults that they were even allowed to try out on the backs of the ponies, many comical situations arose that seemed to increase the general conviviality even more, and that made these two parties for a moment forget that they apparently were rivals of each other. But while Star contently and proudly looked around her, and tried to concentrate on her own work during all the commotion, a voice behind her suddenly sounded; one she undoubtedly had heard before, whether she had wanted it at the time or not...

'Well, you pulled it off, now haven't you?' was what the voice said. 'I hadn't expected a crowd at this scale at all... I have to give it to you, Star...' And an irritating chuckle was to be heard that couldn't come from anyone else than this person. Star quickly turned around to see if this horror had actually manifested itself, after which the boy simultaneously pulled the hood off of his head to make himself known, which made Star's eyebrows raise on autopilot.

'You!!!' Star shouted loudly, at which the boy had to smile.

'It's me indeed!' was what he said in response. 'It's me! The stone statue! The well-read philosopher! The biggest womanizer of Bastion! I'm all of them in one!'

'But…?!' asked Star in surprise. 'And…?! How…?!'

'Just…' said the boy. 'Just… I come in many guises.'

And that wasn't a lie, and indeed a fact, because, even though Star knew this boy as the so-called philosopher, she also knew him as the almost fully masked homeless person who had so willfully wanted to break her idealistic dream picture only a few nights earlier. But since the philosopher could already read her poisonous gaze, he decided to anticipate it right away.

'Look…' said the boy with control. 'I may have been a bit harsh with you that night, but it was only to teach you a lesson.' And he pointed at the multitude of visitors who only seemed to increase in number. 'Lesson number one, Star. If you want to pull off something like this, you'll have to come up with something like a 'marketing strategy,' otherwise it will be a pointless undertaking from the start. And let I just have…' and the boy looked around him, with that haughty, almost arrogant, but that which was also comical, and characterized him so much, gaze

… scattered some of my magic here and there in order to help you along the way…' And the philosopher, whatever his name may be, remained nearby during those remaining successful successive days, and seemed to receive the many accolades, that Star kept dishing out to him, with appreciated pleasure…

Reprisals

The group of Merivians, with Star sort of in charge, had now collected enough currency to be able to stay here for a month, if not longer, and that even in an abundant way, even though that wasn't initially in their intention, and certainly not that of Star. Star's intentions were simply fueled by the earlier enthusiasm that she, when still in Meriva, had put into this plan, and she now finally reaped some well-deserved fruits from that. With a big thankyou to the address of the philosopher, a real popular movement now arose that, from mouth to mouth, seemed to resonate within the deepest and furthest corners of Bastion. And even though this happening wasn't widely reported in the regional media, something that even these Merivians could understand, Star's organized event was nevertheless picked up by some media, simply, because even here in Bastion, an objective form of journalism was still practiced by some; a form of journalism that wasn't corrupted yet, and simply couldn't help but spread news both ways. It was therefore funny to see how a few rickety market stalls, some simple Merivian items and trinkets, and four playful ponies, could serve as a weapon, even though Star would have preferred to depict so otherwise.

The only thing she had hoped and tried to achieve with this fair, was to spread some awareness; to spread a certain realization that would resonate through all layers of the Bastian population: whether it was among the paupers in the slums, among the passengers who travelled high above on the network of rails in some computer-controlled vehicle, or even there in the highest regions of this technocratic capital; among those who made up the laws, forced people to abide by their rules, who executed the destination plans, and who decided whether there should be a network of rails built at that spot at all. The few remaining Merivian items were packed up again, the paupers who had kept an eye on things were given some extra currency, and the group finally set off on another walking trip; towards the exit of Bastion. And even though Star was somewhat wary of possible reprisals against their group, to her great surprise, and also to her great relief, nothing seemed to happen. And so they were just able, and that with a complete pardon, to walk out of the gate of Bastion, to meet up with their two faithful companions who had stayed behind with their now well-fed horses, a bit further on, on the barren plain. They talked long and animatedly about their achievements during the return trip back home, while Star silently and gleefully thought about the words that the leader of the splinter movement had once spoken to her and Thomias a long time ago:

If you plant a seed, a painfully stinging cactus might appear from the soil, or a magnificent growing sunflower of several meters high...

And Star could still recall the exact facial expressions of the man, or even the way he had said it at the time, and there was but one assumption that forced itself upon her, while at the same time thinking of the hundreds of Merivian insights and short stories that now circulated within Bastion's epicenter: *If this isn't going to be a magnificent sunflower, then I don't know what will...*

But Star saw things a bit too sunny perhaps this time, and appropriately so. Because, even though a small popular movement had now indeed emerged within Bastion's many sections, and could perhaps take on even grander forms, she seemed to have forgotten that where people speak openly about such matters, malevolent ears could also pay attention. And moreover, that where a sunflower of many meters high flourishes, thorny weeds can also grow in its vicinity... In any case, the group was welcomed back at the entrance of the hidden valley with loud cheering voices, after which they walked into the green landscape of Meriva with some pride, and also some euphoria.

The group, however, didn't seem to notice that, while they were relieving the horses of their burden, they were being watched from a short distance by none other than their pondering spiritual leader. The man thoughtfully rubbed his chin and then walked away while the following sentence resounded in his footsteps on the shining marble floor below: *Now it's only a matter of waiting for what will come...*

The grandmaster's fear was indeed confirmed. Early the next day, a commotion sounded from the cave entrance; from the vestibule of the hidden valley, whereupon many Merivian guards, residents, but also the grandmaster himself and Thomias and Star, rushed towards the entrance to see what was going on. Two groups of men now stood diametrically opposed to one another: one group armed with sticks and spears, the other group with technologically advanced firearms, with their hands already on the butt of their weapon, but which still rested in their holster in a controlled manner. One man, the presumable Bastian commander, looked up when he saw the unmistakable leader of Meriva approaching, and then walked towards him. An exchange of words ensued quickly; at first with calm tones and fairly shielded from the ears of all the bystanders, but soon more heated and openly; for any bystander to hear.

The commander pointed an angry finger at the grandmaster when the leader of Meriva refused to budge and stood his ground: 'We have all sorts of weapons, old man, don't forget that,' said the Bastian commander. 'And I'm not just talking about weapons made of steel or with pieces of wood mounted on them. Your community has broken rules in several areas, and you know it!' The man pulled out a piece of paper and began to read aloud: 'An unannounced entry into our territory. Illegal residence and falsified residence documents. An attempt at large-scale propaganda and the distribution of propaganda material. An Illegal trade in goods. And I could go on for a while... Let alone the pathogens you unsuspectingly carry with you and unnoticedly have spread within our city. Actually, we should quarantine Bastion completely, and that with immediate effect...' The man snorted his nose mockingly, while his men laughed loudly.

'You know there is only one sanction for this, supposed 'grandmaster', and that is to extradite the person, or persons, responsible for this stirring...'

The grandmaster looked somewhat dejected and tried not to look in Star's way.

'There is one thing I don't understand,' said the

leader of Meriva. 'Why did you go through all the trouble of coming here? Why didn't you arrest and detain this person, or these persons…' and the grandmaster thought he was being clever with this, '…on your own terrain?' But some of the Bastian guards laughed loudly again. 'Are you really that retarded, or are you just pretending?' said the commander bluntly. 'What a great grandmaster you are! Is this your great spiritual leader then…?!' was what he exclaimed while many a Merivian looked at the ground, intimidated.

'Foolish old man, things have already flared up in Bastion because of your previous attempt of spreading propaganda, what do you think will happen if we also tackle the source of this propaganda and commotion? And that under the watchful eye of our own citizens? That is the so-called 'putting the cat among the pigeons…'

'You are also invading into our territory right now,' said the grandmaster in a hopeless manner; hoping for some kind of attempt at recovery.

'You have no written laws here,' said the commander in a harsh manner. 'Only fabrications plucked out of thin air… Our code of law is…'

'…also plucked out of thin air, eventually?' said the grandmaster.

'…is based on…'

'…a kind of appropriated power?' the spiritual leader added again, this time with a satisfied grin on his face. And now it was the group of Merivians who had to laugh at this dialogue, while some of the Bastian guards had to blush a little. However, the appointed Bastian commander was here with a mission, and he straightened his back.

'It's very simple,' the man finally said. 'Either you hand these people over, or there will be an intervention later on and we will smoke them out, together with all the other Merivians...' and the man made a waving gesture with his hand, '...who will stand in our way. The choice is yours, old man, but decide wisely. Because, if an intervention is needed, we will not hesitate to use force...' And the grandmaster was once again put on the spot; yet, another impasse that he could now subdivide with all the other dilemmas that he had tried so hard to cope with, and that for such a long time by now. He looked questioningly and even a little helplessly in Star's direction, who in turn looked at the single Merivian who had joined this heated discussion, and whom she recognized as one of her previous traveling companions. Thomias also looked sadly at Star, after which he saw, and that to his great horror, how she took a big step forward...

'It's me...' she said. 'I'm the instigator of all this disturbance...'

'Good!' the man said immediately. 'Put her in handcuffs! Anyone else?'

'No,' said Star. 'I am the only one who...' But Thomias also took a step forward and held his wrists already together in a somewhat nonchalant way, and he, of course, was also put in cuffs. And without another single question being asked, they were escorted out of the cave entrance of the valley, placed in a large wagon, which then drove away in billowing clouds of dust.

The grandmaster, and many a Merivian, watched with tears in their eyes as the vehicle diminished into a tiny speck in the distance, and then finally disappeared from view; along with the last glimmer of hope these Merivians seemed to possess…

0 or 1 / 0 and 1 / or 100.000.000.000.000

Star now sat in a cold, naked cell. Her few clothes and possessions had been stripped from her body, and she now wore nothing more but a wafer-thin piece of cloth that fell over her breasts and back, that was open at the sides, and that reached down to her ankles. It was freezing cold in the cell and if she wasn't shivering from the cold, that literally crept in from all sides, it was because of her own nerves she tried to keep in check anxiously, but without any result. She should've been thinking about Thomias right now, and even though his name and appearance haunted her mind somewhere, at this point, she could do nothing more but worry about herself. She tried to think of peaceful scenes to temper this almost overwhelming fear, and ironically she found solace in an inner picture of herself; standing in front of that open window of the spiral treehouse that she and her grandfather had inhabited and shared for so long; staring over that vast calm forest landscape that had brought her all the way to this point strangely enough. Star sat down on the thin, flat, and at the same time, stone-cold mattress. She pulled her knees up even higher, whereby she also could feel the cold of the wall radiate behind her, and then started to cry loudly. Not because of her own life, that she undoubtedly would lose soon, but mainly because of all the callousness; because of the coldness that seemed to dwell in the hearts of these Bastians, and that couldn't possibly be warmed up. She curled up into a fetus position, took a few deep breaths through her nose, with all the snot inside that now completely started to come loose, and then just closed her eyes; hoping and wishing that she would wake up the next morning in her own familiar nest, would get up happily to wish her grandfather a good revolution, and then perhaps even go to the community temple in high spirits to kindly, but also somewhat submissively, greet one of the elders to ask for another piece of fool's gold…

She was woken up early the next morning and brought along with much fanfare, and somewhat roughly. Star had started to believe in her own fantasy or dreamworld by now, and whether this had forced itself upon her during her cramped sleep, or just before that, she didn't know, but it was probably due to the shock, because she seemed to repress this entire situation for the most part, and now acted like a small toddler who had just lost her mother.

'May I go now?' she asked in a childish tone. 'May I go back to Alfalfa now, please?' while she tried to look as innocent as possible; infantilely thinking that this would persuade the Bastian prison guard.

'Shut your mouth!' snapped the man. 'I have no idea what you've actually done, or who it is you are exactly, but apparently you are someone of stature.'

Star let it all come over here, while she was being pushed into a cubicle, and with a female guard helping her get dressed. The woman didn't say a word, didn't even look at her, although her nervous mannerism gave Star the idea that she seemed to be afraid of something.

Star was led outside.

She was given black glasses, that prevented her from seeing the outside world, after which the electrical van she was put in started driving...

It took a while for Star's eyes to adjust to the light. The dark glasses and handcuffs had been removed by now and her escorts had, for whatever reason, quickly left again; leaving her all alone in a facility she didn't know or recognize. She looked around a bit, but there was no one to be seen, and the metal door behind her was also locked. She walked a bit further and the environment became more sterile, with steel walls surrounding her, and an immaculate, clean floor below her feet. A hypermodern interior, almost laboratory-like.

Star stood in front of an electronic door with, to her, strange patterns and symbols depicted on it. A marble horsehead statue protruded above the steel door, looking down upon whoever dared to cross this border. The characters

I-II-I-IV-IV-XV-XIV, were engraved on a bronze plaque underneath the statue, but Star had no idea what they meant, or what those strange symbols had to depict in the first place. A hissing sound came from the rubber tubes that ran from above that same door, to under the floor where Star was standing, but the door remained closed. Star touched her chin for a moment, and suddenly a hologram appeared, next to an electronic display that seemed to be the only way for further access.

'Are you familiar with this facility?' the hologram asked.

And Star nodded.

'I don't understand you,' said the hologram. 'Are you familiar with this facility?'

'Yes,' said Star, without lying. 'I've been here for a while now.'

'Are you familiar with quantum mechanics? With Qbits? Elementary particles? With quantum processors?'

Star played dumb, she knew these holograms by now, she had already encountered them several times in downtown Bastion, and it was best to ask the questions herself and let them do the talking.

'Not completely,' said Star. 'Can you tell me more about them?'

'I can only do that,' said the hologram, 'when I have full authorization. Please take a seat in front of the screen, and place your left eye in front of the laser display.'

Star did as she was told and hoped for the best. The display scanned her eye, did its calculations, a number of high electronic tones were now audible, and the rubber tubes that emanated from the metal door made a hissing sound again; as if the door could open at any moment, but not before the hologram had had its say.

'You seem accepted, madam,' said the hologram with respect. 'And you aren't just any, apparently you are of noble or elite blood.

Would you like to enter the next chamber right away? Or shall I tell you in broad strokes about Quantum Computing?'

Star had never heard of such machinery before, but why would the hologram utter it now, at this particular point, if it wasn't of certain importance?

New information was always welcome, and such an opportunity probably wouldn't rise again. Star only hoped that this hologram wasn't as long in content as the many other holograms she and Thomias had encountered during their first visit of Bastion. Star agreed with the hologram's proposition. 'Good,' said the mechanical voice, 'very understandable, brushing up on knowledge always remains crucial, after all. The human psyche is fickle, as we know all too well by now. Okay, where shall I begin, with superposition or with entanglement, or shall I just give you a global summary of the whole thing? Not too scientific, and in broad strokes understandable for everyone?'

'You do that, dear hologram,' and Star had to chuckle a little at the same time. Those digital systems were sometimes quite touching, in a peculiar way.

'Okay, where to start. Let's just begin at the very beginning. Have you ever heard of computers?

'Yes,' said Star, 'but I don't know much about them.' The hologram sighed, 'This is going to be a long one…'

And Star did the same, she kneeled on the ground with her back against the metallic door, with the marble horsehead above her looking somewhat patronizing down on her, while she let the hologram do all the speaking. This probably indeed is going to be a long one…

'Good,' said the hologram once more. 'Let's proceed with the main points.

At the core, at the heart of a quantum computer, lies a quantum processor, and contrary to a conventional computer, it needs a lot of preparation time to get to work. First, the qubits have to be brought into superposition, and entangled with each other. After this, a number of calculations can be performed.

Both the preparation and the reading of the answers will take a lot of time, and the calculations themselves will also be slow. On the other hand, a quantum computer can arrive at the same answer with just a few calculations, where a conventional computer would have to work for many years. These super computers are approximately 100,000 billion times faster than a classical computer. A conventional processor works serially (0 or 1), a quantum processor works only for a short time, but in parallel (0 and 1). They are therefore not suitable for processing in a normal PC, in a smartphone, or in a gaming console, which is a good thing, according to some.

In addition, a quantum processor must be kept stable by all kinds of means, including extreme cooling, but you'll see that for yourself in the next room. Applications that will go much faster with a quantum computer include:

- cracking encryption.
- searching a vast new kind of database with lightning speed.
- in the use of quantum simulation.
- and in artificial intelligence (AI).

The application in a new kind of database is particularly interesting, with all the already available information interconnected, easily traceable and to be resurfaced again. And of course, in the use of, for example, gathering up new types of information, to be put in this vast, enormous, and ever-growing, interconnected network. Opposed to an ordinary bit, which is used in classical computers, a Qbit, or qubit, can actually have the value of two bits at the same time. As I've mentioned before: not a 0 or 1, but a 0 and 1. In physical terms, qubits are implemented in a two-level system, similar to the eigenstates of an electron, a spin, in an external magnetic field.

Not an actual spin, but I'll spare you those details. We are exploring and explaining the workings of a quantum computer here, in broad strokes that is.

Do you want me to briefly explain about magnetic fields?' 'Sure,' said Star, while she banged the back of her head against the metallic door behind her a few times.

'A magnetic field: in physics and in electrical theory, is a field that permeates space, and that exerts a magnetic force on moving electric charges and magnetic dipoles. A few examples of this are: the gravitational field around a celestial body, or the electrostatic field around an electrical charge.

Do you want to hear more about the components of these exceptional machines?'

'Sure, why not,' said Star, understanding about this quantum computing a whole lot more by now, and not feeling much for standing up already.

'As I've told a couple of times before already, at their core, quantum computers rely on qubits in a superposition state, both 0 and 1; a parallel processing of vast information, making them exceptionally more efficient than classical computers. These fragile qubits require sophisticated hardware to shield them from environmental disturbances. This hardware includes: cryogenics, magnetic shielding, and vibration isolation to maintain quantum control of the qubits.

Quantum software, designed to harness the unique properties of qubits, has been devised to exploit the parallelism inherent in qubit-based computation. The development of these algorithms is contingent upon a deep understanding of quantum control, and the ability to manipulate and measure qubits with precision. A quantum processor, or QPU, which consists of multiple quantum bits, also called Qbits, is the fundamental unit of quantum information and is responsible for storing and processing quantum data in a parallel processing way. These Qbits, typically made from superconducting materials, such as niobium or aluminum, are cooled to extremely low temperatures using liquid helium or other cryogenic fluids. This cooling process is necessary to reduce thermal noise and to maintain the fragile quantum states of the qubits.

Another essential component of a quantum computer is the control electronics, responsible for manipulating the qubits and performing quantum operations. These electronics typically consist of high-frequency microwave generators, amplifiers, and attenuators, as well as low-noise amplifiers and digitizers.

You will need a sophisticated software framework to manage the complex quantum algorithms and to control the quantum processor. This software includes tools for programming and optimizing quantum circuits, as well as interfaces for interacting with the quantum hardware.

In addition to these core components, quantum computers often include additional subsystems, such as cryogenic refrigeration systems, magnetic shielding, and vibration isolation systems, which are necessary to maintain the fragile quantum states of the qubits; to prevent them from de-stabilization, so to say. The development of quantum processors, QPUs for short, has been driven by advances in materials-science, particularly in the area of superconducting materials and nano-fabrication. For example, the discovery of high-temperature superconductors has enabled the development of more robust and scalable QPU architectures. Another key difference between qubits and classical bits is their ability to become entangled. When two qubits are entangled, their properties become correlated, so that the state of one qubit cannot be described independently of the other, even when they are separated by large distances. This property allows for the creation of quantum gates, which are the equivalent of logic gates, seen in classical computers.

Qbits are extremely sensitive to their environment, a sensitivity known as decoherence. It makes them lose their quantum properties over time, and behave classically, making it difficult to maintain their fragile state.

This sensitivity requires Quantum Computers, or QCs in short, to be isolated from their environment, which can be achieved through various methods such as cryogenic cooling or electromagnetic shielding.

So... to summarize it in short...

The core component of a quantum computer is the quantum processor unit, the QPU, which consists of multiple qubits, quantum gates, and control units.

The control system is responsible for applying the desired quantum operations to the qubits, which are then measured to obtain the output. And the casing of the core of a QC, the QPU, consists of superconducting materials, nano parts, cryogenic cooling, and electromagnetic shielding devices, to keep everything working and the fragile qubits stabilized.

Do you understand more about Quantum Computing now?'

Star stood up and brushed off her clothing; a somewhat compulsive habit, and quite unnecessary at this point, since this facility was immaculately and sterilely clean. What it had to be, if she understood the story of the hologram correctly.

'I indeed do,' said Star. 'Thank you very much for your very clear explanation!'

'You may proceed now,' said the hologram somewhat coldly, after it disappeared and appeared in several intervals, after it vanished.

Star walked through the electronic steel door, not knowing what to expect.

'Hello?' was what she asked. 'Is anyone there?' But there was no response. Another door suddenly opened in the room she was now in; spontaneously; by what seemed an invisible force. Star walked through the door and found herself in the next one; a room with a very long table, accompanied by two rows of empty chairs, and a flash of recognition went through her constitution. This was a room like she recognized from the meeting room in Meriva, only at that time it seemed much lighter, with more light coming in, and this one seemed more stuffy, almost more dejected. Against the walls stood pedestals with archaic sculptures placed on them; sculptures that she couldn't place at all but appealed to her imagination nonetheless. She stood still for a moment, at the head of the long, stretched out, and also pure black table, a place where the chairman undoubtedly sat, and then looked out over this table towards the door from which she had just come; a door, or so it seemed, that had flung open by its own force. She looked at the sculptures and busts, looked back at the table she was standing in front of, also at the many empty seats, and at the multitude of portraits on the walls, and then sat down in the chair. *And now what...?* But before she could anticipate to this sentence in her mind, a shrill, almost screeching voice was suddenly audible, which seemed to come from somewhere behind her...

'Typical...' was what the voice said.

Star quickly jumped up, turned around, and saw that the large, heavy curtains behind her had been opened, together with the wall behind them, so that a secret passage had now been created. Star walked through the narrow corridor and a figure, in a beautiful shiny red coat, stood at the far end of it, but with her back turned to Star. Currently, there were only six things and objects definable in this narrow tunnel; Star, the fear-inducing figure, a wooden platform with a book placed on it, a small transparent pot with black ink, and a writing quill laying next to the book and the small jar. Star looked at the book and then at the ominous figure standing further away, although the figure quickly raised a hand before Star could even utter a word. As if this apparition had already anticipated Star's potential reaction, and reacted on it prematurely.

'Read...' was all the figure said. Star only had to take a few steps to be able to stand before the wooden platform, and then looked at the book that lay closed in front of her. She looked at the cover with attention, even though there was only one definable image depicted on it; one symbol, one sign, that she knew all too well. It was the image of something she had carried with her all that time, almost her entire life; it was an image of the pendant... The image of a five-pointed star, but on the cover of this book, this image was depicted upside down...

Star was shocked by this, wanted to turn around as fast as possible, and run away as far as she could, although there was also something that held her back in this, plus, there wasn't even a way out to begin with... A voice sounded in the cramped corridor again; only one voice, and only one thought, towering above everything else, while resonating in the back of Star's mind:

Read...

And Star did what she was told and opened the book...

Everything that Star had already experienced in her ever-persevering search for the truth, the many puzzle pieces she had encountered along that long and tiresome road, seemed to form a complete outlined picture in this handwritten book; a schematic layout of all the worlds she had crossed so far. How these worlds were related to one another. And how they directly or indirectly were interconnected. Star continued with the reading, and even though she had the forced idea that this wasn't entirely wise to do, it was also as if she couldn't stop doing so.

The book told her the following points in a broad outline...

The great war; which Star had been taught about from an early age on, was largely a lie. The true course of events was shrouded in shadows and mystery, and the true reason behind it had been distorted many times over. It had become a preconceived story; a means to keep the masses in check and in control, and the true conflict actually raged on to this day, with the majority of people completely unaware of this because they lived in artificial domes...

Star tapped the page a few times with her finger, so that indeed is the case... Even though it wasn't something she hadn't already foreseen. She turned the page and read the following one...

This long-running conflict was ultimately nothing more than a family feud that had gotten out of hand: Two large families, two separate bloodlines, who had stood diametrically opposed to one another for many, many eras, and who both refused to budge or consolidate. And the author of this eye-opening book called these two parties therefore the blue- and the red-blooded...

The blue-blooded ones were mostly put away in set-up domes, after the great and fierce battle that had taken place between these two families, had waged. However, some of them had crossed over to the red-blooded faction, and thus were appointed as wise elders; in order to keep an eye on things, and so that the red-blooded could build their own ideological society; completely cut off from the family branch they had come to disagree with so much while time progressed, and also cut off from their original philosophy of nature's teachings; a doctrine they began to detest more and more. Star paused for a moment, held a finger to her lips, and then had to think of her father's book; a book with the initials *M.B.* depicted on the bottom right of the cover. Star had never known the man's real name, but his initials probably referred to one of these bloodlines, and especially the last letter... Everything was explored in depth in this book: that the elders in the communities of the domes were nothing more than puppets on a string; only a small part of a much larger and higher hierarchy: that of the so-called shadow consulate...

The writings in the book talked of a deliberate, systematic depletion of all life's natural resources, and a striving for a society that was completely dependent on technology. But there was also talked about that which the grandmaster feared so much, and had told Thomias and Star about in complete confidence: a counteracting, or at least an obstruction, of the passage and congregation of souls: a deliberate stagnation of the possibility of merging with a divine higher power that the Merivians had always so deeply and firmly believed in...

Star looked at the last page of the book and then slammed it shut with a hard and also indignant bang. 'Who are you?!' exclaimed Star. 'This is too much! This is too vile! Why are you showing me all this?!' But the apparition had to chuckle and then turned around, at which Star almost jumped out of her moccasins. 'I have been waiting for you Star…' said the ominous figure.

'I can't wait to tell and show you everything…

I want you to be my left hand… Fate has brought you to me... My pendant has brought you to me… I… I was your mother…' Star suddenly burst into tears, and what she most of all wanted to do, was walk up to this figure and embrace it, although there was also something that seemed to hold her back, something that ignited a certain aversion within her. 'But mother…' she sobbed. 'I don't want to belong to the red-blooded… I… I…' And Star burst into tears again, even though she didn't really got a chance to process her grief…'

'Stop calling me that!' the woman suddenly shouted. 'I haven't been your mother for a very long time! I'm something much greater than that!'

'But…?! Star cried out again. 'Why are you telling me all this?! Who are you really?! And why are you doing all this?!'

But the woman smiled mysteriously all of a sudden, and then looked at her daughter very intently. 'That answer is quite simple,' said the woman. 'Because we are evil, Star…'

'Evil?!' cried Star in surprise. 'But where are all the skulls then? The sacrificial table? The many symbols and relics?' Although Star didn't quite know why she brought this up, or how she actually knew about such things. The woman looked at her in surprise, and then quickly burst out in laughter. 'You have just as much humor as your father,' after which she raised her nose in the air in a mocking manner. 'That's all child's play, child. We don't concern ourselves with stuff like that. Not at the top of the pyramid.

We build worlds, only to destroy them again. That's what we do, that's what we are good at...'

Star had a lot of questions by now that were haunting her mind, although strangely enough, she asked the only question that was largely the reason for the starting point of her search.

'But why have the elders always bothered me so much? Have tried to sabotage me in any way to find out about you? When I'm the daughter of a bigwig like you?'

'Oh...' said the woman, without even looking at her. 'Those elders are just puppets, nothing more. You are my best-kept secret, Star. You should have come here on your own accord. That what drove you internally, spirit-wise. A matter of free will, so to say... I want to show you something very important. Go through that last metal door and see for yourself. The woman vanished once more, and Star once again did what she was told and stepped through the door which, just like the previous one next to the hologram, also slid open in a pneumatic way. And from this point on, and without Star realizing it yet, her life, her convictions, and her frame of reference, were set, and would never be the same once more...

Eye in Eye With the Machine

Star entered the room and a massive quantum computer adorned the space.

A huge blue eye protruded in front of the machine, consisting of its molecules, electromagnetic pulses, and ion-fluxes.

Many positively and negatively charged elementary particles, electrons, photons, and ions, swirled through the atmosphere.

'What is this contraption?' asked Star.

'This is a Quantum Computer Star, and there are many like this one, scattered across this world. One like the hologram had told you about, earlier in his presentation.'

'I see…' said Star. 'I think I understand things better now.'

'What do you think you understand, child?'

'I think this is your personal technological network, a means to observe and control everyone, with you at the helm.'

(…)

'You are correct, a vast technological and digital network, wherein souls are being trapped, with no escape, with no possibility to transcend into higher planes anymore, only towards this surface, or into the underground. The universe within a machine, wherein souls aimlessly wander, without a chance of going up, only to remain here, or going down.'

'So your big scheme is to simulate nature and space? Via all this technology?'

'Yes, small child, and this isn't the only system we've put up. You livestock haven't only been put in domes, there's also a vast electromagnetic network put over this entire world, over this entire globe. In this way, the voice of the cosmos, of the creator, of God… However you want to call Him, will be more difficult to hear, even more difficult to receive in the future, with ultimately a certain halt. No more inner speaking, no more chances on salvation, no more way out. Only you, me, and all the beings on this globe and underneath. With me! As your ultimate ruler! As your ultimate God! The upside-down all-seeing eye!'

'God?' asked Star, bewildered. 'Do you mean the universal creative force? Which gives and takes, and that always will be?'

'Whatever you want to call it,' sniffed the woman in scarlet.

'We are playing chess here, remember?'

'Or was it checkers?' Star suddenly uttered, although she didn't quite know why she had said it in that way. The big, blue pulsating eye suddenly became red.

'Where is He anyway!?' said the woman. 'That so-called Great Almighty!? He is not going to save you. Probably too busy with being important, up there above…'

Star was silent for a moment. 'Whatever that force is,' said Star. 'It looks like it is too busy cleaning up your mess all of the time. Working hard to ensure a safe passage for transcending souls, keeping an eye on this dimension, and dealing with you and your comrades all of the time, while trying to keep this world, the universe as a whole, and the dimensions up above in order and in balance.'

The woman in scarlet was silent for a moment.

'Looks like He's hiding.'

'Looks like He has no other choice,' said Star sharply. 'You just want to drag that force into your own chaos, lure him out, to create even more disturbances.'

'He is weak.' Added the woman. But Star had to laugh at this remark.

'Looks to me like He is number 1000, and you are number 999. If you multiply 1000 by 1000, you'll get full circles into infinity. But if you multiply 999 by 999, you'll get even more chaos and confusion. With all due respect, I know by now, that chaos is in your nature, in your core, but it just isn't an order to build an entire universe around. Smaller souls just couldn't cope with such power and chaos caused by you surpassing nr.1. They probably don't even have the capability to comprehend what they've gotten into. It would be far too easy for a mighty being like you. It would be nothing more than stealing candy from a baby.'

Star's eyes were now widely opened, and she also had to sniffle and chuckle a bit.

'This reeks a lot of a marital dispute… And it looks to me like you have a problem with masculinity. Is that perhaps the reason for all the confusing shifting between the sexes? For the uprising of feminism? For the feminization of men, and the de-feminization of women? Let people just be who they want to be, what they themselves feel most comfortable with.

And once again, with all due respect, if you'd rather prefer to curl around another female dragon, be my guest, not necessarily anything wrong with that.

I'm also slightly different in that regard, and whether that is because of nature, nurture, due to circumstances, or all these aspects intertwined, is difficult to tell. But it is what it is, and perhaps an outcome, and due to factors, of having to live and grow up in a dimension like this one. And by the way, I have seen that gleaming marble horsehead outside, watchful guarding the steel door to the meeting room and to this quantum chamber, and there's definitely something going on with him. I can just feel it!'

The big pulsating eye now became even more fiery red.

'It's kind of easy what you do, to be honest. You show no accountability whatsoever, only bringing ruckus, chaos, and mayhem, while others are working extremely hard to keep their heads afloat. There are souls that make the mess, and there are souls who clean up after them. And it takes a year to build a house, but it takes only half an hour to burn it down to the ground completely.

And by the way, what's so wrong with being the second most powerful being in the entire universe? That's a very honorable position, many apparently strive for that, that's quite certain by now. Your many friends and relatives, your other presumable sons and daughters, they would trade places with you in a heartbeat, could they have the power that you possess; by snatching your position away, being the second most powerful being in the universe!' You should be extremely proud of that position, and humbly accept it...'

'Silence!!!' screamed the woman in scarlet, and the room rumbled once more.

'Look around you, child. This is one of our latest and greatest projects. Join us, and we will rule all and all together!'

'I've already made up my mind, mother. We all have our paths to take.'

'I...' said the woman, and the eye flinched and convulsed, and a huge glitch seemed to occur, making the quantum apparatus almost malfunction.

'I...' stumbled Star. 'I... I love you too, mother. I really do. Despite everything that has occurred in the past. Despite all the immense suffering, of all of us.

And nr.1 loves you too, probably most dearest of us all. Return home with us, please. Let's be one great family again, all of us...

And I am very proud to be of your blood, but...'

A big roar trembled through the atmosphere, and a moth and a butterfly fluttered through the room for a moment, swirling around each other, after dropping dead on the floor simultaneously.

'I have heard enough. Go now!!'

The meeting room was suddenly packed with men;

those who called themselves the red-blooded, also known as the so-called shadow consulate... A group of very shrewd characters who, for a very long time, had been busy building their own ideological world behind the scenes.

These men had wound up in heated conversations, and even though they were aware of Star's presence, it was also as if they were completely ignoring her. As if she wasn't worthy, or allowed, to be among them.

As if they in advance had known of her personal decision not to want to function, or play a part, within their shadowy ranks.

Yet, Star could still catch a crucial word here and there, with some of these men glancing at her briefly from the corners of their eyes to gauge whether these topics of conversation had any effect on her. But Star finally knew the bigger picture by now, and even though she knew she had to choose her words carefully among this crowd, she also felt a certain anger igniting within that she just couldn't control or temper anymore.

She looked briefly at her mother, then looked at these high-ranked gentlemen with fire in her eyes, and then, with a certain stateliness, pressed an index finger on the shiny black table, which immediately caught everyone's attention.

'You may be evil!' shouted Star. 'And evil may have its right of existence in this world! But there is also something as balance! It's never enough with your kind! You go way too far! Even entities like you must know certain restrictions!' Star took her finger off the long and also mirror-smooth table, after which the dropping of a pin could be heard. The men at the table looked at each other for a moment, then looked at Star's mother, finally looked at Star again, after which they promptly burst out in simultaneous laughter. One of the men stood up and pointed back to Star with his own powerful index finger.

'Whaha! Ignorant girl! 'Politics isn't for children! You've made your choice, and that's fine, but we'll never be like you! Never!!!'

Star looked at her mother for a moment, and even though she looked the other way, she also nodded in agreement with this saying. Another tear rolled down Star's cheek, even though her grief was in vain, and apparently wasted on these kinds of entities. Star was led out of the meeting room by her mother, the outer door was unlocked again, after which, and to her great surprise, she was released. She turned around for a moment and looked intently at the only mother she once had, that she had just met, barely knew, but knew quite thoroughly at the same time. This time, the woman looked back harshly, as if Star had betrayed her trust, as if her daughter had deeply disappointed her.

'But mother…' said Star again, whereupon the steel door between them slowly closed, and whereupon one more remark was audible between the tightening crack… I have decided to let you go…

'Go and wander, child. Go and wander in that plant world of yours, just like your father has always done…'

'Yes mother, Star replied, and you go wander in your technology and space then…'

Everyone Goes Their Own Way...

Star had been put on dark glasses again, was probably put in the same wagon, after which the vehicle escorted her back to the gate of Bastion with slightly buzzing sounds. She was roughly taken out of the van, put back on the streets, and with a request whispered in her ear to never ever set foot in this stronghold again. She walked out of the large, wide entrance gate somewhat disillusioned; the gate which connected this modern, progressive, technological world with the barren and desolate natural landscape outside.

On one hand she was intensely happy to ever see the light of day again, on the other hand she was disappointed because all her previous efforts seemed to have been completely in vain. Her personal vendetta against a power bloc that was much larger in scale, and much more powerful, than she could have ever imagined; always forcibly pushing forward, and that without any concession whatsoever. Star walked a bit further. Now, there were about thirty meters between her and the stronghold she had to turn her back on, if she wanted or not. There were dozens of kilometers between her and the hidden valley, and perhaps hundreds of kilometers between this point and the artificial dome she had once called her home. She stood still for a moment, characteristically held a finger against her lips, and then thought carefully. Hadn't she forgotten something...?

'Thomias!!!'

She quickly turned around and gazed at the immense gate entrance in the hope that her companion would appear at any moment, but there was no one to be seen of course. She turned around again in disappointment, took a few more hesitant steps over the bone-dry ground, after which a voice suddenly sounded.

'Star!!!'

Star turned around, completely overjoyed, after which she saw how Thomias, without any form of guidance, walked out of Bastion's gate.

'Thomias!!' she loudly shouted again, even when he already and almost stood in front of her. 'They... they released you...?!'

'Yes!' Thomias also exclaimed happily, and with a big smile on his face. 'Somehow, and when I mentioned your name, they just let me go...'

And so the two stood opposite one another for a while, not really knowing what to say, or where actually to begin with their story. Thomias decided to ask the question that mattered the most at this particular moment; a question that would shape Star's life in the near future, and beyond.

'And what's your plan now, Star?' Star looked over her shoulder, over that barren and deserted landscape, and then shrugged. She then looked with sadness at the greatest friend she'd ever had, and she probably would ever have again. She had so much to tell him...

She knew almost everything about this world by now, although, and knowing all too well, she could never discuss these topics with him.

Thomias, in turn, limped a bit on both legs, sometimes looking at the ground a few times, and then with a blushing face at Star.

'Star…' he said calmly. 'I want you to know that I… I… I would like you to know that, I…' But Star already walked towards him, hugged him firmly, and then gave him a passionate kiss on his mouth.

'I have to go now,' she said. I can't stay here for much longer. I'm no longer welcome here.' Thomias smiled briefly, then nodded, even though he didn't quite understand this sudden course of events.

'What are you going to do now?' she asked Thomias, whereupon he also looked briefly at Bastion and then looked back with an even bigger smile on his face. 'Well… I think, Star…' he said calmly, '…that it's about time to become a real inventor…'

'But…?!' exclaimed Star in surprise, after which she looked once more, and with big frightened eyes, at the high fortress of Bastion that towered high above everything else, although she also had to smile. Thomias shrugged his shoulders amiably. 'I'll catch up with you soon Star, in Meriva.'

After which Star walked onto the barren plain solely, and Thomias himself towards a city he had actually always dreamed of.

The two turned around for a moment, looked at each other in silence, after which they probably would see each other never again. However, an intimate bond of deepened love between two young people that probably would always continue and persevere, and that one often only encountered in epic tales like this one.

Star walked on for a couple of hours, and Bastion had almost completely disappeared behind her, and from sight. Multiple dust clouds and low humming sounds were suddenly audible, and various black vehicles appeared closer and closer, before they completely encircled Star.

Star could now do nothing more but await her fate. She was glad that Thomias didn't have to witness this, and he would probably never hear about it.

The car doors abruptly and simultaneously flung open, and then everything went to black, with only one thought of Thomias fluttering out of Star's existence.

Of course, I love you too, you big numbskull!

Epilogue

A tale of Love and Lust?
Or a battle between Love and Lust?

Some say… that from the very first beginning of the apple, to the utmost end, it has all been about *Love and Lust.* And perhaps that's why this is the most difficult dimension to tackle. A universe consisting of two opposite poles—a clashing of two great families who once were one. Lust… a part of the 7 deadly sins, opposite to the 7 eternal virtues. A 'sin' so difficult to tackle, because it can also contain, and be derived, from Love; Love and Lust combined; an inescapable derivative of the natural reproductive drive. A force so strong, that even angels struggle with it, while demons use it to their advantage.

A mighty dragon with 7 heads, not willing to give up this aspect of power, and *Who* is almost impossible to undo from this cosmic impasse.

Perhaps it indeed all started with Love, and was Lust—the symbolic apple—that dangled seductively and with temptation in between, like Damocles' sword.

Perhaps this pandemonium indeed transpired because of the Love that the human male and the human female can feel for one another. And perhaps also, because higher beings, higher deities, with all their extraordinary powers, can feel solitary within this aspect, and become jealous of this higher cosmic phenomenon. If the great celestial dragon indeed has 7 heads, roaring as a bewildered lion, but more so, howling as a wolf at the full moon, or perhaps even hissing like a reptile, then this lust-aspect will indeed be the most difficult downside of the universe to overcome. And that's why some are of the assumption that this is the last dimension to be purged from false ideologies, false egocentrism, and false projections. In principle, a Love and Lust dispute that number 1000 and number 999 just couldn't work out in some way, and amongst each other, with angels of light, and demons of smokeless fire, in the midst of all this, and with the creation of humans—male and female alike—as an ultimate effort, as ultimate evidence, how Love between two souls could truly feel. An ultimate effort of number 1000, to express His Love for number 999.

An extremely painful effort to show His Love to Her, with almost infinite sorrow and traumata in its wake, still very palpable till this day…

Will the love eventually be in vain? Or could it eventually be returned in all of its grace? Is this indeed the last dimension to be conquered? And is this indeed the last battle to be waged? In the very end, only time and space can tell…

The grandmaster of Meriva

There is no intuition greater than that of a Star…

About the Author

Rambaro Pellegrino; author of *The Chateau*, and now of this next novel: *Bastion*.

Born to a Dutch mother and an Egyptian father, and raised in a historical port city named Hoorn in the Netherlands. A city which stood at the cradle of the New World. A place not that hard to find, one only has to cross the pond.